the grammar architect

Also by the author

The Inactivist

the grammar architect

chris eaton

implosion
imprint

INSOMNIAC PRESS

Copyright © 2005 by Chris Eaton

All rights reserved. No part of this publication may be reproduced, stored in a retrieval system or transmitted, in any form or by any means, without the prior written permission of the publisher or, in case of photocopying or other reprographic copying, a license from Access Copyright, 1 Yonge Street, Suite 1900, Toronto, Ontario, Canada, M5E 1E5.

Library and Archives Canada Cataloguing in Publication

Eaton, Chris, 1971-
The grammar architect / Chris Eaton.

ISBN 1-897178-05-0

I. Title.

PS8559.A8457G73 2005   C813'.6   C2005-903424-6

The publisher gratefully acknowledges the support of the Canada Council, the Ontario Arts Council and the Department of Canadian Heritage through the Book Publishing Industry Development Program.

Printed and bound in Canada

Insomniac Press
192 Spadina Avenue, Suite 403
Toronto, Ontario, Canada, M5T 2C2
www.insomniacpress.com

HALF, THE FIRST

Burke and Micheline

I. A blank page, and other white surfaces

IT WAS ONLY a matter of time before Neil offed Judith.

To Burke, it was obvious. The signs were all around him.

The connections:

#1: that winter, the temperature dropped so fast that the lake froze practically clear. The ice was over a foot thick, and you could still see straight to the bottom.

#2: that winter, the temperature dropped so low that the air was congealed with the sounds of splitting trees and telephone poles. The veterinarian had never seen so many shattered hooves. If you dared to put your ear to the ground, you could even hear the muffled pops of crackling bones in the graves beneath the old church tower.

And #3: that winter, at the supermarket near Burke's apartment, they'd installed devices in all of their shopping carts so that the wheels locked up when they were pushed beyond a certain perimeter, and the parking lot was surrounded by these errant, crippled carts, like an army of malfunctioned, robotic horses, making it near impossible to manoeuvre your truck. The bag boys abandoned their regular duties to retrieve them. But the carts refused to come back into service. And when the snows came on so suddenly, they were forced to abandon them like childhood dreams, or unwanted pets, and the frozen lot was transformed temporarily into a landscape of frozen glens. A white so pure and untouched that it seemed boundless. And entirely without depth or surface. Or movement.

As white as habit. As white as a nightmare.

As white as a beginning.

And how the rest of the story fit together was for Burke to discover. Trying to capture the overall ambiance of the moment through abstract pieces of the whole. He even showed up at the crime scene itself: the empty apartment where Neil and Judith had lived together for several months before both of them disappeared from his life forever. It was empty except for the occasional nail in the wall; a shoe box full of outdated computer manuals, warranties and old boot-up disks; some half-empty paint cans under the sink; closets full of accumulated hangers. Not a smoking gun, perhaps, but evidence of a sort. Of course, by the time he arrived, the police had already put up their yellow tape, and the detectives with their long coats refused to let him by.

"*Pas de lieu Rhône que nous,*" the Chief Inspector joked. And they all laughed.

When Judith and Burke first met, she tried to tell him the story of her first real boyfriend, the Dutch dye tycoon whom she'd witnessed murdered at the hands of a competing cartel. It was the reason, she explained, that she was so afraid of the snows that winter. One of the first connections. And after listening intently, he merely responded by quoting Poe: the truth was that life was lacking in "the pungent contradiction of the general idea," which was to remain believable and yet be extraordinary. Life was not worth living because it didn't make a good story.

It was either unbelievable, like her story.

Or it was boring, like now.

II. Birth of the Grammar Architect

THERE WAS THE story of Judith and Neil, true love interrupted periodically, like the broken distress signal of a sinking ship caught in a hurricane, by Tragedy. Before they met, their lives were so quiet and solitary. As solitary as death. But possibly a death that comes from a plethora of life. Through friends of his parents, Neil had found a job with a construction company to fund the novel he was working on. But it took him nearly ten swings to drive home a nail. And he could not be trusted with power tools. So his job often amounted to retrieval from the cube van. About three weeks into it, while closing the rusted vehicle's roll-up door, the wheels caught on the guide track. Without letting go of the handle, he leaned in to strike the track with his hammer, and his right hand was crushed when it was torn into the upper compartment. Rather than have him go on government disability insurance, thereby increasing their own monthly payments, the contractor simply agreed to pay him in full until he was better. And when they received the job to restore the old church tower, they told Neil he could work as the "Project Historian," documenting everything he could find within its walls and describing everything they had done for posterity.

Judith, who'd only just arrived in the City before the winter struck, found it all fascinating. This writing thing. It seemed amazing that something as simple as words had the power to transport two people—writer and reader—to a completely different time and place. You know? She wanted to know where he got his ideas, what his influences were, if he wrote in a straight line or in disjointed chunks, and if the girls she'd read about in his first books were based on any sort of reality or just pure creations of imagination. She hoped for the latter but might have forgiven some of the former. Try as she might, though, she could not get him to talk to her seriously about it.

"It's hard to describe," he said when she finally cornered him at the Grad Lounge. He was stuck in a stalemate chess game with the painter, Marsh. She was leaning over his shoulder.

"Like a sibling?" she offered.

"More like a rock."

"Solid and mysterious?"

"Unshapely and boring."

Sure it was! And what was his new book about? "Oh... well..." And here, he suddenly lost his focus on the board in front of him, looked down, looked embarrassed.

"Archways and reliefs, candles and dustballs, shards of glass, wine stains, this and that..."

Which was when she decided he was making fun of her, suggested a move he had not seen, and left him sitting there wondering what he'd done wrong.

"Fuck," muttered Marsh, rising for another beer.

And Burke was there to write it down, the look Marsh gave Judith on his way to the bar, a connection that would not seem important until the story of Judith and Marsh. Then again, when he really started looking at it, every relationship was important. And here was the making of Burke's first list: *The List of Romantic Connections, Real and Imagined.* There was the story of Judith and Neil. But also Marsh and Dallas, another real deal; Marsh and Judith, a deal become real; and even Marsh and Isabella, the Art History major with hair like a cloud of blackflies, who showed up on the first day of classes without a place to live, when Marsh gave her a spot on his futon. On which he also slept. There was Judith and Burke (which wasn't much of a story, really, when it came right down to it), Burke and Anne-Sophie, Anne-Sophie and Judith, Anne-Sophie and Nästa (the pimply cellist no one ever got to know, including the mob who caved his skull in). And then there was Dallas (the beautiful physicist who would disappear and leave Marsh wondering for the rest of his life) and her ex-boyfriend Ymer; Dallas and Booting (who was also part of their group). Judith and Venn. Judith and Booting.

And every story looked the same.

At least at first.

III. "If only more of the specifics were known..."

THE STORY OF Burke and Micheline was different. More or less happy. It involved models and cigarettes, supplication and rejection, like the stories that involved Marsh, and beautiful shades of brown and red like Judith's—but also fierce hallucinations that chewed at his hair, and someone who was willing to deal with his neuroses, his obsessions, his habit of poetic waxing. He was literally at the end of his rope when she found him, so upset by everything that had happened, eating toast for breakfast, lunch, and dinner. And she brought him back from the edge. Somehow the poet and the model fell in love.

"And I felt as though I knew her," he told Marsh about his vision, the one who had been visiting him in his dreams ever since he hit puberty. Not that she looked the same, mind you. Her hair was a different colour, for one thing. And he'd never quite imagined anyone so tall. But one had to be adaptable. "It was just that she gave me the same feeling of... you know... comfortable complexity. You know?"

But if Neil was their voice, then Burke was just a dreamer. And Marsh was their wisdom, able to hold sway over most any crowd using only his indifference. This was the reason Burke came to him in the first place. His words, his gestures, and his manner were all unfocused yet profound, with a dizzying ability to say and do nothing at all to the point of exhaustion:

"The dead are to be mined like any resource," he would remind them. "For words, or knowledge, or beauty, or carbon. Anything else would be wasteful and negligent..."

Or: "The love of novelty is the cross of sympathy, and demonstrates a naïve *je m'enfoutisme*. It is a transitory, positive sign without a cause..."

Or in the case of Burke's latest story about falling in love with a runway model: "Not everybody's beautiful, Burke. Not like in your little world."

"They could be."

"Who would want to be?"

It was queer, certainly, how out of touch Burke seemed to be. He was living in a world of his own, and there had never, ever been anything like it. Never could be, in Marsh's opinion. It was too beautiful altogether. When Burke showed up at his loft to talk about it, the painter wasn't really even sure what to do with him. Unfamiliar with the formalities of entertaining male guests at his studio, Marsh offered him wine anyway, lit some scented candles, put Beethoven's *Für Elise* on the stereo, and pretended to make sketches in a small, suede, handmade book he kept near the bay windows so that the light from the street lamps outside would silhouette him as he worked, his hair blowing in the teeth of the wind. The divine artist, sexy as hell, worked like a fucking charm. Burke had to shield his eyes—he held his tape recorder awkwardly over his brow—to see him properly. Then Burke started going on about lists, and "meaning," and "the unimaginable prize of complete understanding." His life, he claimed, was no longer in order. Life, he realized, was just a long series of inconvenient coincidences. But he also wanted so desperately to figure it out. Problem #1: art. At their parties, Burke squatted in the kitchen and mourned the passing of individualism, hoping his persistent resistance to depersonalization might save them all, simply yearning for the first and greatest of all artistic dreams, something commensurate with his capacity for wonder, the orgiastic past that year by year grew more distant from them, to create something original, something alien to the collective consciousness. Problem #2: his memory was failing him; to the point where he sometimes forgot the names of his parents, or Micheline's, his ATM code. Problem #3: he often felt the urge to throw up, and sat still for ten minutes at a time until the feeling subsided. And Problem #4: just as Burke's understanding of the world had already become suspect, his mother "murdered herself."

"It's not that simple," his father tried to rationalize.

"It can't really be classified as a suicide, not in the normal sense..."

One of her personalities had decided she'd had enough, and had starved one of the others to death.

Schizophrenic rivalry.

His father chose denial, insisted on something rotten. He shook his head sadly when the book of mug shots failed yet again to produce anyone with the likeness of her murderer. And his lawyers, through a number of loopholes and verbal-legal gymnastics, maintained the case indefinitely, even now. But Burke was an intellectual, with the mental capacity to understand complex emotions and concepts and to translate them into art. He studied technical psychiatric texts and first-hand accounts of patients suffering from multiple personality disorder, as well as books on phrenology and alternative healing methods. He wrote and presented papers on the fragmenting effects of creativity on the North American psyche. And he composed poems with words and concepts like *anthropocephalic chancres, dementia praecox, perceptual paresis, hebephrenial derision*: poems filled with multiple voices printed one directly on top of the other. He expected it to make him a household name. Overnight. Yet despite a reasonable success with his first chapbook, his publisher seemed to have lost interest in him ("The winter of our dissed content... har, har, har..."), and they decided to pass on it.

Life had become Burke's enemy without him knowing it.

His depression grew...

...and developed into philosophy: The key to getting through Life—beating it—was to think like Life, to get inside Life's head and anticipate any move before Life made it. Keep one step ahead of the game. To do that, Burke had to understand Life completely. And by studying the rest of them—by introducing more objective distance from the subject—he thought he might better be able to understand himself. So he gathered every available object they were known to have touched and catalogued them, creating elaborate lists that he hoped might provide some clue to his purpose. Anything could be the key to complete understanding, even the drink in his hand. What had Marsh said about booze? The artist's *ami*, or *âme*, or *amertume*, or something like that...

The results, however, were distressing.

"If only more of the specifics were known."

Of course, the simple reality was that bad things happened. Or, rather, things happened, and sometimes they were bad for you. You just had to figure out why they were bad and somehow you might remedy that problem. *Why?* was the key. He knew everything they'd done over the past year or so. But so many of their decisions seemed without sufficient motive, chosen randomly, as if controlled by some malevolent outside influence. And without motive, it was as if none of it had happened at all. *Who*, *What*, *When*, and *Where* were easy to establish. Contemporary forensics had managed to take most of the fun out of death. Out of mystery. Through DNA, Fingerprint AFIS, the FBI, and any assortment of other letters, they could piece together the logical sequence of events that led up to Judith's premature demise. And they could undoubtedly link it to Neil. But without a motive, could there really be a crime? *Murder* was definitely the ontological cause of *being murdered*; because X had been murdered, an act performed on X by Y, X must also be dead. But without the *Why?*, they were missing the First Cause. The reason for the story in the first place. Which meant they were left with nothing. Without a reason. A stage of logic was missing from the sequence.

So he started re-examining the lists, searching for those connections, drawing diagrams, cross-referencing his cross-references. And when it had become too confusing to flip back and forth in his little red notebook, he switched to speech cards that he could spread across his dining-room table and even staple together when the links were clearly established. Linked cards were pasted to the wall, so he could stand back from them and contemplate the bigger picture, which also facilitated the addition of future links. Unlinkable cards were to be kept in file folders in a small plastic lock box he had inherited from his parents for storing receipts.

The file folders remained empty.

There were no unlinkable cards.

With Marsh peering over his shoulder, Burke

attempted to outline his findings, the events which had transpired to bring Judith and Neil to this impasse: "The tower, Neil's book, his job, Judith's father, that time travel guy..." Oh, hell... Didn't Marsh see it? If he could figure out what had happened with Neil and Judith, he might even be able to put his own life in order, perhaps even figure out why Dallas would decide to leave Marsh so suddenly when things seemed to be going so well. Surely there had to be a reason. Things didn't just happen through cruel twists of fate. Everything was connected. And if he could just get into her head, they could know. Marsh could know.

"You know?"

Then Marsh, vehemently, vatickly: "Psychology has nothing to do with reality, nor should it be used as motivation."

...which put an end to that.

IV. A depressing scene

AT THE WAKE, leaning on Micheline for support, Burke threw up in the wine cistern, and took up oratorical duties in the sitting room:

"...and her lips, her lips were like twin rose petals, red as rubies, a bee-stung Singapore sunset, my swollen heart... o cunning Love, with tears thou keep'st me blind, lest eyes well-seeing thy foul faults should find..."

But Burke was younger, still a poet. Everyone understood, and forgave.

"I feel like I'm separating," he said later, in the car on the way home, meaning not that he was full of so many different personalities like his mother, *per se*, but different opinions, never quite convinced enough to make up his mind one way or the other. He had so many goals. So many dreams. He couldn't fathom how the rest of them did it, succeeding every day to choose a clear and precise direction through life. If things were bad now, what about the other, inchoate tragedies of life? The weight from unclear potential outcomes crushed him into inaction.

When he was at his worst, Micheline held him tight, tried to squeeze the "other thoughts" out of him, but there were times it seemed he didn't even know her. He just sat there on the edge of his bed going through some old notebooks and weeping.

"Something's missing," Burke muttered cryptically, not entirely sure what that thing might be.

And she nodded, because she was beginning to think she understood him better than he understood himself, and because he needed her support, and because it was all you could do when he talked like that. She suggested that it might just be the season. The changing pressure. And although his poetic mind barred him from seeing anything so simply, it did not inhibit him from overlooking this ontological simplicity in others. So when he saw how she was trying to reach out to him, he wanted to at least look like he was reaching back.

"It makes moods insurmountable," he offered with a shrug.

Yes! That was it exactly! Purpose was the slave to memory, and memory was the slave to the seasons. And when summer dragged itself from the earth, carried on the wings of those pesky June bugs ("O God, when they get into your hair..."), Burke would invariably drop this crazy need to prove things, perhaps to write another play. Summer was not a season for quests, but for lounging in the sun and drinking sweet wine coolers on the back porch with friends. Maybe they should take a trip. To

England? Surely there would be few tourists at this time of year. But the rain! And what with the exchange rate being so poor nowadays... Might it even be boring? Thus the afternoon: they forgot all about Burke's being sick in mind and at heart, and all about the universal encroachment of death. Instead, they discussed what was proper for the spring: bumblebees and caterpillars, new loves, circus freaks, Tragedy...

Meanwhile, Burke was actually just comparing his own mind to the graveyard ("Have I resorted to metaphor?" Burke scolded himself softly, shaking his head), full of dead plots, tragic heroism and such. This and that. Something else. The small grubs pulsing beneath the bark of the leafless trees and the gasoline rings skimming the green-brown puddles. The gravedigger's shovel leaning irresponsibly against the tombstone of the brilliant cathedral architect, or critic, or young girl, now pleasantly composting beneath the surface. The snow—what was left of it—had dumped itself into small clumps like acne on the Earth's backside. Just snow? Or, hiding underneath, some part of the Earth normally obscured from the human eye. An invisible cancer which only manifested itself at the end of the life cycle, in winter...? If Neil had really knocked off Judith, then the rules were tossed out the window. Bodies in motion became bodies at rest, and the energy that had existed in Judith's life disappeared without transference. It was never recovered by anyone, certainly not Burke. Neil and

Judith were Burke's voice and his body, and when they carted Neil off to the big house, Burke retired to the study, silent and invisible. To the lovely, diamond-cut Micheline, he said: "They have taken everything I have. Abandon me in the snow where I can crystallize into something more blissful and useful."

Luckily, Micheline's practicality was such that it was adaptable, absorbing Burke easily into her designs, but it left no room for second thoughts, or for abandonment to the elements. She told him to grow up.

He would get over it.

"Never!"

Then he could go screw himself. She had better things to do than try cheering him up all day.

And the force of Micheline's departure sent one of Booting's sculptures crashing to the floor.

"You'll never understand, babe!"

But how could she? Micheline and Burke shared everything like any other couple, meaning they spent most of their time together while keeping certain things silent. Her interest in whatever. His interest in something else. Her short affair with Marsh. His need for Judith. She cared for Burke, needed him, desired him. So close to love was their relationship that it pained her to hear him, through the wall, raging methodically into his portable tape recorder. Burke's despair was such that he blamed himself for Judith's end. Burke's nature was such that the set of his reactions was predetermined by poetic notions of justice and grief. Micheline listened to him attack the pillows she had scattered on the floor near the fireplace, beat his chest, rummage through the drawers of the cabinet next to the settee, and curse the walls that he could find no paper to make note of his torment. It made her curse with him. Was there no God?

But Micheline got him talking, involved him in the dissection of what she had said ("The result of not having lived enough, I suppose..."), what he had said ("Perhaps not entirely accurate, but insightful..."). He crossed to the bay window, traced his fingers in the rivulets of condensation on the glass. What did she think about love? Who was really to blame? Micheline's solutions did little to assuage Burke's apathy, or his guilt, but they succeeded in distracting him from his next logical plan: self-determination: killing themselves together: an alternative with which she hardly felt comfortable.

"Nice night for a walk," Burke said, shutting the door before she could follow.

The coast was hard and wet, and a bloom of dark purple cast seemed to exhale from the shoreward precipices like smoke from a cheap cigar. A coastal crag; an empty street. It was at times like these that the coast seemed its most bleak. The gulls, long accustomed to tourist feedings, panhandled even in the winter despite the fact that it would kill most of them. The grass was dead. The sand was hard. And on the brow of one hill, of rather greater altitude than its neighbour, stood the church, which was perhaps the cause of everything, black and bare, cutting up into the sky from the very tip of the hill, its square mouldering tower, owning neither battlement nor pinnacle, of one substance with the ridge, rather than a structure raised thereon.

It was more like the story of a tower, and its graveyard, serrated with the outlines of graves and a very few memorial stones. Not a tree could exist up there: nothing but the monotonous gray-green grass. And the waves at Burke's feet... a wave was the cursed soul of a sailor lost at sea, lunging desperately at the beach, nearly reaching dry land before being sucked back into the ocean, spent and frustrated. Burke remembered telling Micheline that story when he had first brought her here. Sure, sweetheart... that's the fate a man's got to wake up to every morning and still manage to climb in the boat. He missed the times when things were that simple.

Without Judith, he was doomed to hover like a lost soul, only barely touching real life before being sucked back into nothing.

Over and over...

The whole aspect of the scene had that depressing effect on Burke which few places can produce like the beach on a winter Tuesday, when it's raining, and you feel as though you are in a detective novel, and nothing makes sense.

Burke and Anne-Sophie

V. 'Melodious bird, sing madrigals'

ANNE-SOPHIE'S THROAT had always been her most prized possession, as opposed to the other little girls who clutched their virginity tightly to their puffy chests. At the age of twelve, when puberty brought her up to a towering five-foot two-inches, and she made it successfully through the *Queen of the Night* aria for the first time, her German vocal coach had shaken her nearly senseless, then tied a kerchief around her neck with so many knots that she couldn't undo them herself. "Zis vill be vurth more zan your *la-la*," she was told, meaning her vagina or her virginity, she wasn't sure which.

Regardless, she gave them both up a few weeks later to an eager thirteen-year-old who practically came on her stomach before he could enter her, on the back steps of her best friend's porch, his scrawny French body weighing heavy on her pelvis, the splintered ridges of the steps digging into her back. She'd need regular massages for the rest of her life. He bypassed kissing her neck entirely, pushing as many fingers as he could into her dry, unwilling *la-la*, and when he eventually entered her, each boring, abrasive thrust was like sand between her toes. Thank God he came so quickly, she could just be done with it.

It was hardly the last time one of her lovers would bypass her high G-spot entirely for the certainty of his own quarter-note spurt. But it was not until much later that she would discover her vocal instructor had been right all along. Even without the fame and fortune brought to her by her legendary pipes, it was her throat that she would eventually prize above all else. As a young girl in Paris, she had only *Emmanuelle* films to coach her, and so she figured it was just a matter of time and travel before the orgasmic spasms started racking up. It was just a matter of working it in. Or maybe finding a position that was suitable to her. Yet her vagina remained as insensitive as a journalist. Her nipples might as well have been callouses. She tried just about every pianist from Vienna to Japan, hoping one of them would have the magic fingers to find some erogenous spot on her. But she entered adulthood without once reaching a climax. Or even a first movement. A symphonic swell. The excited splatter of the brass section clearing their valves.

Not even when performing solo.

Even Gene Simmons, with his fabled prehensile tongue, did little for her down there. They met during the recording of *Pavarotti and Friends: for the Families of Failed Time-Travel Experiments*, where Simmons and

Pavarotti collaborated on an orchestral version of "Beth," and Anne-Sophie battled it out for prodigal supremacy with Charlotte Church on a rocked up *"Komm heraus"* (the "Jealousy Duet" from Weill's *Der Dreigroschenoper*). She'd never felt better. Bending her notes around that British poser made her vocal chords vibrate so much she started to tingle. In fact, she was even in the mood give it another try when she found the KISS frontman waiting in her dressing room. After about an hour of Gene's salivary basting, however, she squirmed out from under him and headed for the door.

"Hey, hey, baby, hold it now, that's not what women do when they get the deep KISS, you get me? The fella needs a little reciprocal action, alright. Now, let's do us both a favour and climb aboard the love engine, cos I've been stoking to be stroking, and hey! Johnny! shit, stop that bitch before she— no, Jesus H. Christ, Johnny, don't come in, I just— she— fuck, Johnny, I mean, no it's too fucking late now, isn't it, she's already gone, just go find me that Church broad, would ya..."

By the time she met Burke, she'd all but given up on the idea of achieving an orgasm. She still took the occasional fan backstage after the show, whenever she'd discovered another position she hadn't tried, but her heart was rarely in it. When she removed the kerchiefs around her throat, even her biggest fans recoiled from her strangely. On her North American tour, she decided to drop the whole thing.

She met Burke at gunpoint, during her continuous marathon performance of Wagner's entire *Der Ring des Nibelungen* cycle. The early rushes raved that Anne-Sophie's portrayal of Brünnhilde was more spectacular than Nilsson's, Evans's, or even Dvoráková's. A must see. And so opening night was packed rafter to rafter with all the City's elite and culturally force-fed. Of course, they left the performance not understanding so much ("It was what, you say? In German?"). But the set was so beautiful, and most sat through it because it was something to talk about at next week's parties. How could you deny the force of something so audacious as opera? It was so... remarkable. There were some, however, who did leave early. All those blond braids and Viking horns made Dallas—she was still unknown to them all at this point, visiting on the recommendation of her thesis advisor Dr. Wonmug, who thought it might be better if she took a short leave of absence from her studies until everything settled down back home—think uncomfortably about Sweden, and she kacked out before even the first act was over. At the first intermission, only two hours into it, complaining bitterly of "some wicked shits," Neil abandoned Marsh, Isabella, and Burke and took in the rest of the opera from a tavern around the corner where the acoustics were much kinder on his ears. And Marsh, whose insides were also inclined to the delicate side at opportune moments, excused himself soon after, ignoring the glares Isabella sent after him.

"What?" she snapped, staring at Burke. "I'm supposed to stay here with this moron alone?!"

Booting never came at all. He said his dick was too sore from masturbating, and claimed "those fat opera chicks always give me a woody." Plus, he regarded opera, largely, as part of the problem. These classics. These artistic canons. Even through artistic revolutions, the Modernist screen of Revolution had been placed on the Dadaist screen of Revolution, on the Victorian screen of Revolution into perpetuity, and the holes had all been filled by constant layering. Art was destroying itself through mundane repetition like muted, ominous drumbeats. Becoming mass-production. The past was preventing the present. The only way to avoid despair was to destroy everything. Forget everything. And start again as if it were Time's very first second.

If he was anything, Booting was probably their vice. Or their anger, although they each carried a little bit of that around at most times. Somehow—and possibly this was because he'd grown up in a home of folk artists, with a father who played classical guitar in church every Sunday and made hand-made Celtic bodhrans in a shed behind the house, and a mother who sold various arts and crafts at the weekly farmer's market—he'd ended up working in stained glass. At university, he was immediately set upon by the other Fine Arts majors for working in something so antiquated ("What happened when the glazier discovered there was nothing new to be done? He lost his temper! har, har, har...!"). They were relentless in the way that only the snobbish can be. And while this certainly pushed the perimeters of his work into sculpture, and inspired him to explore the possibilities of windowed glass without lead lines, the various epoxies and other adhesives he used achieved only minor success. They worked fine with smaller pieces but couldn't maintain their integrity for a full-sized window. And after three years of the same jokes ("Get it? Temper? Har, har, har..."), he gave it all up and turned his skills to installation and performance.

...which was partly why he'd purchased the antique pistols in the first place, at an auction to raise money for the work they were doing on the new church tower. Up to that point, he'd merely pantomimed throwing up on paintings in public galleries, retching loudly as he disfigured them with vials of paint in all the primary colours. He lit small fires in the enclosed spaces of automatic banking machines. But the guns were part of a plan to start destroying all of his past work. To erase it forever. *The only real form of creation left is destruction*, he wrote in his first manifesto. *It is making things not be, but it is still making things something.* ...which was better than the uneducated itching powder the rest of them called art. Duplication without information. Borrowing techniques and images without context (what he called photocroppying, or photocropping, photocrapping). The spirits of Jarry and Tzara were on his artistic doorstep like flaming bags of shit. And he cursed the rest of them, especially Neil, for being "propagators of the universal catechism." Neil was working on a new book, a list of objects, sensations, and boring, outdated conceits—no plot, no conflict, no characters—that would make up a building, a tower; a novel constructed out of stones, support beams, altars, ants, dried sperm, dust, pencils; the critics were hanging on its arrival like snot, waiting to be blown away.

"And even that's been done before."

When Marsh and Neil appeared at his door, however, a bottle of rum in each hand, they lined up all the pieces he'd gathered so far at the other end of the yard, and then blew the fuckers to pieces along with a good portion of the fence. An artistic preview, of sorts. The mother of the children playing in the adjacent yard came shouting obscenities, accusing them of trying to murder her kids, to which Marsh decried that she was standing in the way of art, and would she please move before he had to call the police.

"If you please, *ma-da-me*, you are obstructing clear progress. Destruction is the natural course everything must follow. We are only speeding up the process somewhat. If you would like to be next, I would be perfectly willing to oblige."

"To think and to dethtroy!" Neil cackled distractedly.

And there they stayed, firing tiny pebbles at the bare legs of the children (they'd run out of real ammo long before) and reminiscing without shame, so that nearly seventeen hours later, during the final act of Anne-Sophie's North American debut, Neil burst on stage with a mask covering half of his face, and a pistol in each hand. Screaming slightly off-key, he announced himself as *die fliegende meistersinger*, let out a tremendous fart, and pounced deliciously towards the lovely little soprano, Marsh and Booting aping along behind him carrying spears. Anne-Sophie, the smallest woman ever to play Brünnhilde, tripped over her own braids, crashed through a *papier maché* boulder, and fell squarely into the lap of the poet in the front row.

Burke, who had never seen the French chanteuse in his life until that night, fell in love immediately, as was his nature. Her hands lingered on his shoulders as she got to her feet, hands so cold and white.

"I think I love you," he whispered as she pried herself loose.

"Alright…"

VI. The opera

AFTER THE PERFORMANCE, Burke lurked backstage near the dressing rooms. With chocolates, roses, and an intense longing. Hoping to catch a glimpse of her. He was enraptured with her, with what he saw as her unquestionably Hollywood lifestyle. The unattainable *op*-star. She met his advances with some reluctance ("*Merdre!* That crazy guy is out there again..."), but Burke, who was not averse to rejection because he bathed in it every day, who knew that oppression of one sort or another was the fuel of all great art, refused to give up. He was also occasionally endearing, and Anne-Sophie admired his determination as only the French can, eventually granting him the prize he sought—her—if only for one date. Something public, but with plenty of alcohol so she wouldn't appear terribly awkward; and at the end, a peck on the cheek and a fake phone number. So easy.

Fortunately for her, when he showed her off at Marsh's party for Neil, her English was not good enough to know that they were mocking her. They considered themselves real creators, not just people who presented another person's work ("Sure, it takes practice to hang paintings, too..."). Plus, rumours of her life had preceded her, and it was already being insinuated that there were other things she could do with those fiercely developed throat muscles besides singing. Booting asked her if she ever thought of doing "the movies," which she appeared to consider before replying that speaking only strained the voice. The endless repetition of lines might do her career more harm than good. Booting, who thought she might be flirting, trailed her to the kitchen for another drink: "Actually, I was thinking of movies without too much dialogue." He pushed his tongue several times against the inside of his cheek. "You know. Action films..."

Only Marsh attempted to make some amends for the interruption of her show (Neil made it a rule to never apologize), first making attempts at pleasant conversation ("That song you sang in the second act... no, the other one... yeah, well... wow..."), and then just plying her with drinks when he realized he had none of those light familiarities of speech which, by judicious touches of epigrammatic flattery, can obliterate that tone of complete disdain or boredom. Not that he cared so much about ruining the show, but it was simply in his nature to flirt. Thankfully for Burke, his play at friendship gradually brought her out of her shell. She accepted drink after drink. And, surrounded by the group of them off the kitchen, she began to speak of other pieces, other things that made her heart rejoice or were important for other reasons. Her thoughts and her opinions. Like North American food, or movies, or even the opera they had just seen:

"I must disclose I hate Wagner," she admitted privately to them, over-Anglicizing the composer's name to impress them, "but I can no longer endure any other music."

"Naturally," added Booting. "What a shortstop, I mean, Wagner, wow, that Flying Dutchman stole seven hundred and twenty bases in his career! Not too many bow-legged fat guys could do that, I'll wager!"

Then Marsh: "Wagner sums up modernity. There is no way out. One must first become a Wagnerian."

And Anne-Sophie: "But I enjoy also Schoenberg," she cooed. "Some of the times."

And Marsh, who'd really had enough: "Ah, yes, surely one must then become a Schoenburger."

Only Burke, with his intense poetic desire to be loved, or at least to create the illusion of it, praised her without hidden slander. All this despite their obvious incompatibility. His poetry was an attack on her ears, a barrage of hissing noises that characterized the English language for her. About Philip Glass: "An opera in English? *Impossible!*" For some reason, she had this real hate-on for Charlotte Church. For him, conversely, her music was so limited ("The alphabet has way more than eight letters, you know..."), drowning in its own repetition and its statements of the obvious. But Burke saw these immense differences, their incapability to conduct any form of real communication, as intriguing, almost cute. Anne-Sophie said so little (which was a precursor, of course, to his relationship with Micheline, who only said things with her body) that he thought she was just shy, perhaps awed by him: the brash, artistic North American. He was lonely, prone to any relationship that might one day lead to nostalgia, and so he built it up.

"Her voice... bites at your eardrums... whistles through your hair... parks itself inside your rib cage and strums... strums your spinal chord..."

His love was the love of poetry, not in-depth musical critique.

The one thing they would eventually share was Judith, although Burke's connection with her was more symbolic and prolonged—a professional longing, it might be said—while Anne-Sophie's was more fleeting, yet real and transformational. Burke had been boring the soprano all night with his interests and hobbies, descriptions of his latest work ("Something semi-autobiographical, I think, but with the driving force of motif..."), and more than once during their glorious evening, drunk from close proximity and nervous tendency, he began to recite Dante to her in Italian ("*Amor, che al cor gentil ratto s'apprende...*"), botching his translations irreparably: "Lamoor that of gentle breast rathe is intaken." Did he think she wouldn't know? Unable to deal with him any more, she sent him on a wild goose chase ("Yeah, Marsh might have some Grand Marnier around here some-where..."), planning to slip away quietly.

Then, suddenly, there was Judith. At this point, no one even knew her name, just knew she was hot and drunk, and had stolen most of Marsh's rum. She confronted Anne-Sophie near the stereo, barely coherent, dragged her into the middle of the room, started swaying; and the music, although uninspired and much too heavily bassy, was not entirely unpleasant, and actually shook Anne-Sophie's whole body, so that she realized there was something, mmmmm, somewhere, ah-hahhh, that was registering, oh! and it was just a question of locating it, stroking it, touching it, Judith's delicate fingers tracing lines along her face and shoulders, pulling her close, and...

Oh, mon dieu...

Anne-Sophie described it later as if a cloud had descended over her, grabbed her by the ass, and slid a knee into her crotch. But what she didn't include was the cloud's finger that somehow slipped through over two dozen knots and traced a line along her neck, causing the muscles to buckle and reach out, pulsing with new life. Suddenly, the tongue in her mouth was no longer enough, and she bit relentlessly at lips, tongue, shoulders, nose, earlobes, popping the clasp on one of Judith's earrings and sending it chiming down her vocal apparatus. Bells rang and whistles blew—this time only figuratively—as piece by piece of Judith's body tickled the roof of her mouth or the back of her throat, and she came without anyone even touching her fabled *la-la*.

She was only vaguely aware of everyone else in the room watching her as she took one of Judith's fingers into her mouth, swirled her tongue around it, took it deeper...

"Who's the piece?" Booting spluttered around his cigarette.

"What'd you say her name was, Burke?"

Burke, who knew so little about love, and so little about everything else that was important to him, which was everything, did not feel free to comment.

Anne-Sophie, meanwhile, felt the first tug of the earring catching in her oesophagus as Burke ushered her out the front door, mistaking the slightly nauseous feeling for love. And that night, with the heady rush of Judith's finger nestled in her throat, Anne-Sophie took Burke home, her breath hot like a space heater on his chest and neck. ("I just kiss it," she blistered into his ear, sliding down his torso to where, surprise! surprise! things were really happening!) He was probably already comparing her tits to sparrows, and her la-la to a summer's day. (Damn poets! Always making more out of Life than was really there.) But he filled the space in her more than music did, and so, for the moment, he was good. When it was over, she wrapped her throat in elaborate scarves with terrible knots, but not before Burke saw the first ripple, like a worm burrowing just beneath the surface of her skin, bulges most frightening because he could not understand them.

"What do you want to eat?" Burke asked apprehensively.

"I don't know," Anne-Sophie said. She had a voice like a trumpet. Metallic. A dame with brass lungs. "What do you want to eat, Burke?"

"I don't know," Burke's eyes narrowed. "I don't know what I want to eat."

Outside it was getting dark.

VII. General turmoil

IT WAS A season of love, as winter is so often wont to be. The snow came in on mysterious trucks overnight, great plows that piled the rabid stuff by the side of the road while they were all sleeping, barricading them in their houses, and surprising Burke and Anne-Sophie into thinking they might be meant for each other after all. It was so cold, and he was so warm. It would all be so much easier to end it in the spring, if and when it ever returned.

She was his inspiration, his prom-dressed vision, his fuse. He blamed their poor communication not on incompatibility, but on faulty wiring, on the fact that his personal *parole* did not match with, was not the same voltage as, her own Pidgin English. It was certainly not her fault; English itself could no longer adequately express the feelings he felt for her, anyway. And she could hardly be expected to pick up on every subtle nuance of his speech when he had made such a practice, such a pride, of English mastery, and she had been raised on the Romance languages: French, Italian, German. English was an offence to her ears, like a steaming history of piss and shit.

Burke wrote a series of poems around that time, forty of them, dedicated to her. They retold the events of the flood, but instead of rain this time, God sent snow, an arctic froth with drifts like sagas, deep as Burke's thoughts, and banks filled with nothing but the blank cheques of new possibility. Adam had named the beasts of the land and air, made them words, and Adam's scurrilous beast-words were kept alive and conjugating by the ark, the first floating dictionary, compiled by Noah and his brutishly practical sons. They were the first censors, attempting to cleanse the world by removing language's four evils: slang, homograph, fantasy, and profanity. But as Noah's middle son Ham warned:

"You can't have animals without fucking."

"We shall see," Noah replied. "We shall see." It was this repetitive speech impediment that had led to gathering two of every animal. "Bring me a stork," he ordered. "Bring me a stork." And they brought him two storks, which caused the whole "f-word" problem in the first place. Noah tried to keep the boys and girls separate, and the animal revolt began as the first flakes of snow began to fall. Noah's tongue was pressed to the metal mast by the monkeys so that he couldn't speak; Shem lost his speech to frost-bite, and his words fell blue from his lips; Japheth was gored through the throat (Burke's subconscious attack on Anne-Sophie?) by a unicorn (hurray, fantasy!); even Ham, cursing like a sailor, went down in the confusion of *tough cough* and *hiccough*, *though thought ploughed through*, snowy sparks hailing from his stormy jaw. Thirteen million words obliterated by ice, replaced by nothing but snow, repacked into a new language. With numerous references to the Inuit. Crystals forming star(e)s and le(tt)ers, and wor(l)ds and idea(l)s, and whole poems in the (s)mash of his (s)mittened hand.

"*Blue words and thoughts*," it ended, with Ham abandoned in the snow, his body crystallizing into speech, "*charred remains / freeze her burn / and a voice clear and hircine / which was when he saw the vision: ashes to ashe* *o *she* ** **he*...*"

And then another forty pages filled with nothing but asterisks.

But the reality was that Anne-Sophie and Burke were not meant to be. They were in love. Just not with each other. Of course, that mattered so little at the time. Instead, they shared a common muse, and projected their image of Judith on to each other, putting up with the other's personal traits with all the gallantry of the newly coupled. His poems became more sentimental, more lyrical, more epical, more dramatical, and she pretended to read and enjoy them. She sang songs without choruses, without a beat, in languages he did not understand, and he looked up from the newspaper and applauded demurely when he thought she might be finished. He made dinner for both of them, and she pulled on rubbery, yellowy gloveries to do the disheries; he brought her walnuts, and she cracked them open inside her throat, coughing up the meat (what happened to the shell, he was never sure...) for both of them to share.

But then:

"What about coming back to my parents' house for the holidays?" Burke asked her.

Short silence.

"We should talk."

And general turmoil. There was someone else: a turtle-necked musician who was making a name for himself across the City by destroying his cellos at the end of his performances. Their conversations shifted from weathery non-committals to direct attacks on the things they valued most. Her vocal training now drove him crazy ("Haven't you nailed that fucking scale yet?"), smashing her notes against the bedroom wall, plonking those horrible canticles in the kitchen ("Serves me right, I suppose, for screwing a Catholic..."). And she was equally sick of him tracking his poems like muddy feet through the house, drunk with the Past's ideas ("Demarker!"), scribbling as if he were dribbling, pissing his hissy words all over the toilet seat, and the sink, and the walls, and all the way down the fucking hallway ("Your poems you piss all over me, *espèce de petite crotte...*"). He was afraid, she said, of trying to make it in the real world, to bring the people something they could use or want, was wasting his time with a dead language like English ("...perhaps not full dead, then, but full of the disease, sterile from so much over-fucking..."), a Germanic language become the language of the germs.

"And this Jojo-violin-dog-boy of yours... do you really think people want to see a guy in crotch-cut tights set his nuts on fire while he plays? Or watch you unscramble a Rubik's Cube only to have it tossed up sick and sinusy? It's disgusting."

"Your poems are like stink."

"Beautiful. What the fuck is that supposed to mean?"

"*Tu te fous de ma gueule!*"

"Right back at ya, baby!"

She was no fucking muse. She walked with monosyllabic steps, tripped over the allusions and wordplay that he lived and breathed. He was better off without her.

VIII. The break up

FOR ANNE-SOPHIE'S part, she continued to feel that tug in her throat she could not explain, never quite sure if she were experiencing feelings for him or—possibly— the residual effects of too much second-hand smoke. Certainly it seemed to her as though this other boy really understood her, could at least assimilate what she told him and produce the proper response, which was more than she could say for Burke, who assimilated very rarely, and responded almost never. And the whole thing came to a close after a fight they had about the correct pronunciation of Nike.

A: "You just can't accept the fact that I'm right!"

B: "You can't accept phonetics!"

A: "*Espèce de salaud...!*"

B: "Bike... trike... like... hike... mike..."

A: "*Tête de lard!*"

B: "Dyke!"

Strangely, it was in Judith that Burke took solace from his break up with Anne-Sophie. She was having similar problems with Booting, whom she met at a similar party one week later, in the basement hallway, the stained glass artist no more than an inch from her face, when he'd said such nice things to her and she went home with him because at least he wasn't making fun like the rest of them. Now she was feeling directionless, as if perhaps she'd made a wrong decision somewhere and ended up at this dead end, this quicksand, this reiteration of habit.

"I'm not sure what I'm looking for, Burke, what I want to be, or who— it's like I've had all this potential my whole life and I have nothing to apply it to, and it makes me feel guilty because it looks like I'm doing nothing... You know?"

He did. When Anne-Sophie finally left him for good, he gathered every person, place, and thing Judith was known to have touched and began cataloguing them, cross-referencing his cross-references, forming elaborate charts that depicted the connections between all objects, but the results were distressing. No reasons, no excuses, no whims, not even any theories. No way to get closer to her. Instead, he dwelled on beautiful, untrue things, the place she held in his creative pantheon, how he considered himself no more than a worshipper, a poetic historian like Homer, and was thus defined by his relationship to her. He had the privilege of a bit part in someone else's story. His life was without sufficient narration of its own. It was Judith who made him what he was, the body who brought out the words in him. Without her, he was nothing.

"And maybe there isn't anything?" she was still speaking. "Maybe, just maybe, there's no real reason to try at anything because it all brings you to the same pointless goal. Right?"

Right.

"I just always feel like I'm missing the boat on something, like I'm missing out. And I guess that's the reason I keep going from job to job and place to place and person to person, God, I feel like an idiot sometimes, just like, I don't know, like I'm missing something... Just missing something..."

And Burke didn't say that he was also missing a few things, some answers, didn't express his true feelings. When he ran into Anne-Sophie by accident one day, and she asked him if he was still writing, he shot back, "About what?" and refused to look her directly in the eye.

"Really, Burke, you're starting to creep me out..."

Ha! That was a laugh. *He* was starting to creep *her* out? With those planetary pipes of hers? Get a load of yourself, baby! This world's a crazy, mixed-up place, and sometimes the only way to pick your way through it is to pick a target and keep firing. You and me, kid, we could go places, take this world by the privates and make a private place for just you and me...

"You'll find someone," Judith assured him.

And he tried to picture her naked.

Judith and Booting

IX. 'Twas on the evening of a winter's day.'

JUDITH WAS BORN out of Booting's spreading forehead, which was split open by greed and lust, not to mention pain. Where others saw finished beauty, Booting saw potential. Transparent character: flashed glass. Armour: shine and solid malleability. As far as Booting was concerned, the others were pure amateurs, still working with dead materials. Here was a real body to mould. They had no vision. He set aside everything else he was working on, and set about creating her. As with most of his other projects, he talked about it more than actually doing anything.

"What you pathetic pukes haven't yet realized is the potential of the body. Watch." Booting held his hand over the lamp. "See how the light shines through the fingers. Without flashing, you can't get glass that red, normally so goddamn dark it looks black, and no amount of grisaille will ever produce that shading. Could a sculpture ever reproduce the scene of a teenage boy thrown clear of the wreckage that was once his car, a rib puncturing through his chest at the nipple, his knee bent backward, and his face staring into the black hole of his own ass?

The hair sprouting from a mole? Real bodies, real art. Like those robot guys who perform on street corners, fuck, yeah... And dancers! Have you ever seen dancers? What they do with their bodies?"

They all ignored him.

"What I could do with a fucking dancer!"

Judith wasn't a ballerina. No. But the way she moved. Grace. Poise. And what was it? Hilarity?

"A. Piece. Of. Art! That, you fuckers, is the future!"

Neil blew a smoke ring. Marsh chuckled as he sketched the two kids in backpacks at the bar. But Burke was enraptured. He hung on Booting's every word.

"Fuck, Burke, are you taking notes? Jesus Christ!"

And he crossed the Grad Lounge to the tinsel-mouthed folksinger by the jukebox:

"So, what's it like to kiss a girl with braces, anyway?"

"Some guys find braces sexy."

"No, no, I was actually wondering if *you* had ever tried it..."

But the women around the Grad Lounge all knew Booting by now. Knew not to trust him. And if they didn't (the new ones, younger and younger every year, every day), the waitresses at the Grad Lounge soon warned them.

He stopped tipping for his drinks.

Things looked bleak.

And then, suddenly, there was Judith. She showed up at one of their parties wearing a knit tank top and floral pants, berating Neil and Marsh for a discussion they were having about women's beach volleyball as the true athletic/artistic symbiosis—and, therefore, symbol—of the contemporary Olympic Games ("Who the fuck are you?!"), grinding by the stereo with a petite soprano named Anne-Sophie (Burke's date, whose throat was already insured for a tidy sum, but only a portion of what its talent and size would one day require), and giving them all the worst case of blue balls in their lives before eating half the leftover turkey in the fridge, downing most of Marsh's rum, and gravitating to the settee where she remained for the rest of the night, silent and unfocused. They observed her from the safety of their drinks in the doorway.

"Who's the piece?" Booting spluttered around his cigarette.

Which was all they needed to get started on her. Marsh felt she was hopelessly *bourgeoise*: young, angry, and dressed like a hippie; he would have nothing of her. Burke, who was a bit dismayed that Judith had kissed Anne-Sophie before him, did not feel free to comment. And the others just couldn't get enough of her. There were so many questions: Who had invited her? Where did she come from? How could it be that none among them had ever seen her at the library and fantasized?

She was new. And perhaps lonely.

Even Burke's date—the French opera singer Isabella made them go see ("God forbid you idiots should experience anything that doesn't involve explosions or car chases...")—could supply them with nothing. To her, it had been like a cloud had descended over her, grabbed her by the ass, and slid a knee into her crotch. Whenever she tried to think about it, she became lost in her own thoughts. She tugged at her lip. "We did not talk about things."

No. Of course not. And they despaired of ever seeing her again. But then, one week later, Booting was talking to her in the basement hallway, amazed at his own luck, no more than an inch from her face, his hand softly stroking her cheek, whispering all the crap he thought she wanted to hear:

"Are you kidding me? Hands like yours and you're not a sculptor or something? I don't mind telling you, I'm surprised..."

And Judith, who'd only been in love once before (with a Dutch dye tycoon by the name of Venn), and had never had the benefit of that love turning sour (such a tragedy... to die so young...), was entranced. She was so new to this place, knew no one. And Booting seemed nice enough, cute enough. He seemed so obsessed with her hands, and his were so strong and sure, the way he pulled her fingers apart, tracing with his own fingers the slight webbing between them (a deformity inherited from her mother). When he held one of them over the lamp, it felt warm and slightly erotic, like a dry tongue pressed against her palm, or the heat of the sun that day in Paris when she'd first met Venn in the lobby of the Hotel Grand. She was sure these two kids with backpacks were tailing her from the *Musée Grévin* (she'd secretly attended the unveiling of her mother's wax replica in the sports section), so she ducked into the hotel for cover. As luck would have it, it was the day on which they exchanged the spring plants for the summer ones, so the lobby was practically bare, but one young man dressed head to toe in red noticed her plight and came almost immediately to her rescue.

"Are you being followed?" She nodded. He handed her a vial. "Rub this into your hands. It's an ultra-absorbing compound I've been working on that will be soaked into your skin and spread to the rest of your body in seconds. Then stand by that wall over there until I get back."

"But how?" she asked him when he returned, in the elevator up to his room, after she had kissed him so passionately in the lobby. (The other patrons and staff watched Venn paw frantically at the air around him, until finally he was asked to leave.) It made no sense.

"The human eye is an imperfect instrument, Judith. Its range is but a few notes on the real chromatic scale." Venn was conducting these experiments in his off-white laboratory in Holland (a beige so faint that it was indiscernible to most eyes, maintaining the illusion of sterility, but just enough tint to subdue his albuphobia). He was in Paris only to find investors. "If colour is the refraction of light rays back at the eye, why can't we turn those light rays back around? Force them into an endless loop of chromatic paradox? It's what you might call invisibility, but really it's just creating colours we cannot see..."

Thank God he had more of those vials in his room, rubbing them on each other this time, unable to find each other except by touch, hoping an arm was a leg, that ears might be lips, wow, Venn would touch her and withdraw, touch and withdraw, coming at her so quickly she briefly thought there might be four of him. Maybe there was, she hardly knew the man. She stayed with him for years, picking up his sense of colour, his intense, irrational fear of white, and screwing like dust storms nearly every night with her invisible lover, the full weight of another body she couldn't see, a pressure between her legs, and a feeling of being blown up like a balloon...

"My place isn't far from here," Booting was huffing into her ear.

Mmm-hmm...

But outside, winter had struck without warning. The seemingly organic streets had grown a fine layer of cold, white moss. And the spores from this icy infestation had jettisoned themselves into the air as well. Spreading. Reseeding. Choking out the life-giving lawn greens and brick reds, this flood of arctic froth. It was horrible to her, sickening, this layering of nothingness, blank canvases across the entire City. For reasons Booting never would have understood anyway, she was afraid to leave the safety of the cab's blue vinyl interior, if even for a second. All he noticed was the way she buried her face in his shoulder. The warmth of her breath against his ribs. She didn't think she could make it, she told him ("What?!"). Not through that, no, not through— God, she felt like some delicate pink-flowering thorn, oppressed between winter's blank pages...

"Sure... all... right... look, if you need me to I'll carry you all the way up there myself..."

And when she opened her eyes again, she was once again surrounded by lovely, horrid wallpaper, so rich and confusing to look at. She felt safe. When Booting returned from the bathroom ("Can I get you something to drink... a beer, maybe, tequila... holy fuck, thank you, God...!"), she was already rubbing some of his colouring agents across her stomach, her pants around her ankles, her exposed buttocks like blown cobalt, the dreamy sky heroine of his every fantasy. Here, at last, was his perfect human canvas. He guided her to the bed, told her to lie down, and brought out his cartooning paints, charcoal, that bottle of tequila, transforming her into various saints and prophets, the entire Resurrection Mausoleum (in segments, of course, but all two thousand four hundred and forty-eight of them), the Five Sisters. It was there, in the apartment above the Bauer's garage, that Booting remade her like so many stories, over and over, at first just copying what he'd seen in reproductions on the Internet, then gradually inserting more of his own designs. Licking her spine with blues and greens. Massaging the charcoal nub from heel to inner knee. A wave across her shoulder blades. Popping the lid off another paint can and thrusting his brush into it, over and over. Judith arched towards each horsehair touch, lying on her back as though the wind had tilted her, black lines separating each colour, each section of her body, bucking and moaning, fingertips breathing against the cool metal curve of the other open tins. She was so solid, unbreakable. She inspired him like no one else. On the last pass, however (he was re-sectioning her again, oooh, tracing new black lines with his charcoal tip across the worshipful scene of her rear and inner thigh, yumyum), she stayed his hand, told him *exactly* the way she liked it. Nothing left uncovered. But also no black. No absence of colour in any sense.

...which inspired him to return to his quest for a glass that would make his fortune: a borosilicate-type substance that would hold its shape indefinitely without the aid of cames. Booting had already returned to stained glass via Neil's construction company, as he landed the job as designer for the new tower windows, but if he could perfect this process, he'd be more famous than any of them could ever have imagined.

And there Judith stayed. For months.

When they discussed it over bridge, no one could understand it.

"One club. Is she blind?"

"Or stupid? Pass."

"What can I say, fellas, I guess some girls are just attracted to a big cock."

"I'm sorry—one heart—maybe I missed something, but I always thought you were a big ass?"

"Har, har, har, laugh it up while you can, punks, but I am telling you this girl is double-jointed in all the right places..."

"Two hearts," Marsh bid, dropping it.

Judith became an obsession for all of them. She possessed an air of naïveté that so obviously accompanied a great lay, and an air of mystery that spoke pretty much the same thing. Hips like an Inuit sculpture. A waist like time slowly passing. Tits like tits.

And, as Marsh finally admitted to the rest of them, she had lips like a cherub's ass.

"She's all cherub ass," Booting responded.

It was Burke—silent, pensive Burke—whom Judith took into her confidence: "I mean, Booting's different and all, but..." By which she meant that he wouldn't fail to shock her parents ("Or somebody's parents..."), but that she also found it difficult to live in the world Booting had supplied her. He rarely cleaned; the kitchen, which he also used as his workshop, was splattered with piles of coloured sand (really various metallic oxides), stale bread, jars of silicon dioxide, mustard stains, hardened wax, greased-up dishes, and a spare pontil. And that didn't bother her half as much as the couch, the silverware set or the lamp filled with marbles, the crucifixes and Biblical quotes, the bed placed directly opposite the door ("Hasn't he ever heard of Feng Shui?"), everything furnished exactly how it had been when he moved in seven years previously, a university freshman with crates & crates of *Dungeons & Dragons* modules, posters of British New Age bands he never fun-tacked to the walls, and limbs that were still too thin for a normal adult. He refused to believe that his environment had any effect on him, and so he left all inanimate objects exactly how he found them to prove a point. From what Booting had told them, when Judith made an attempt to change things, he changed the locks. She spent an entire night on the wooden stairs brushing excited earwigs from her legs, and was still happy to see him when he opened the door the next morning.

"How do you put up with him?" Burke asked her.

"Well, the good times can be really good..."

Yes.

Plus, Booting's perverted accounts fell drastically short of accuracy. Her decision—or rather, indecision—to stay, her locomotive stasis, was due more to the weather than anything else, the horrid drifts that continued to dog her as March gave way to an even snowier, ungenial season. The snowstorms that visited them in April were grander and more terrible than any she had ever seen before (the coldest on record throughout the northern hemisphere), lasting far into July, September, October, by-passing summer entirely and going straight into fall, and she fell quickly into despair. Here she was, trapped in the Arctic wasteland of her nightmares, nearly surrounded by ice, which closed in the garage apartment from all sides, scarcely leaving Judith the space in which she floated. She tossed full cans of paint from the kitchen window ("Hey, that stuff's expensive...!"), bailing it over the aluminum sides, but the snow only covered it with whiteness, momentarily erased it, left her with only the dissipating hope of colour shadows. And eventually even they faded into white. When she realized that it wouldn't end for months, she gave up, accepting that the only way to ride this storm out was to stay where she was, begging him nightly to reapply the colours she felt might save her from the blankness that surrounded her.

Booting had, of course, fallen in love with her. It was the unavoidable consequence of Judith's proximity; just one of the tricks and traits she inherited from her father. But Booting was the first, if you didn't count Anne-Sophie, whom none of them really knew, or Burke, who was a poet and fell in love daily. And despite the stories he told the rest of them, Judith and Booting never even slept together. He was too afraid that any push towards further intimacy might scare her away. Around her, in fact, he was a completely different person. When it was just the two of them, he barely even swore. He brought her anything she needed. Most of the time, he just sat on the other side of the room and watched her in silence.

The true story about when she offered to help him around the place: he wouldn't allow it. But not because he cared about the space. He simply didn't want her to feel burdened. To grow disillusioned with the affection he sometimes thought he saw in her eyes. To ever think of him as something that takes effort. He didn't want her to leave.

Truth be told, Booting wasn't her real problem. She was just missing things. "Love, I guess, but, but more than that. Have you ever felt like you're not really you? That some vital part of you has been destroyed by your past? Ah, what a poor nobody I am!" she said, sighing. "People who go about the great world don't care in the least what I am like either in mood or feature." What she was trying to say was that she was not an artist. She had never created.

"Oh, Burke, what will I do?" Her hopes and aspirations spilled out of her, collecting slippily around Burke's feet, making it difficult for him to stay up. Her desire to be an artist rather than art, her environmental concerns, her drive to be independent. He attempted to understand her, associating her with the proper stereotypes. She shrugged her shoulders, understanding that was the way men were.

And it was during one of these recurring storms that Judith first saw the monster ("At least, that's what I thought you were," she would say to him later, "that first time..."), his feet cold and blue, the beginnings of his fabled manuscript hidden in his haversack, the backyard lit up by the moon's reflection off the fresh fall, the pines made visible. There was a scene, illuminated for an instant before the snow fell again, of a young man kicking the crap out of his bicycle (she thought she'd seen him break four spokes!) before the storm carried him from her view. And as he listened to Judith's description of the antagonable snowman, Booting's spirits dropped.

"You mean Neil?"

"Is that his name?"

Judith and Neil

X. A whirlwind romance

NEIL WAS A writer. Which meant he wrote more than just emails or office memos, ad copy or term papers. Song lyrics, phone messages, postcards, or notes. He wrote more than just articles, pieces, or poems. More than just tickets, speeches, or tomes. Library request forms. Short stories. Or even just scrawling things on the wall of the bathroom, although he was also known to participate in that.

Once, someone had written the date (could it possibly have been that long ago?) along with the words *I WAS HEAR.*

Neil took out his sixty-nine-cent BIC and added *WEAR?.*

It was strange enough that he and Judith even ended up together. When she first arrived in the City, she was in no state for another relationship. Cripes! It was one thing to break up with your boyfriend, quite another for him to fall to pieces right before your eyes. She was slipping through life as if she were sleeping, barely reacting to the many courting advances paid her by the surrounding artistic gentry (which honestly made them all want her more, drawn on by her colossal indifference). Neil had spent years mad at the world, practically demanding the first kiss and then abandoning the relationship for dead. He pursued relationships like meaning. But the pillow talk always left him wanting, oppressed by sticky sheets and uncomfortable familiarity, turned off by their tastes in movies, books, positions. Or, as was more often the case, they just couldn't deal with a nutbar neurotic like him, who spoke so little sometimes because he was preserving every word—or so they thought—for his magnum opus.

Judith and Neil's, however, was a whirlwind romance. They agreed to meet downtown where the lights of the bargain stores would lend them both some extra glitz, and when the street kids approached them for money, they dug deep, as if to say: "Money means nothing to me compared to the experience of being with you." A subway token. Coins dropped in a mittened hand. Listening to that old harmonica guy play that one note over and over was well worth five bucks! Oh, yes! They both feigned embarrassment at being late, for not immediately recognizing the other ("There were so many women with long blonde hair, I felt like a drowning sailor..." "And all I could remember was that you weren't, you know, bad looking, I mean, I agreed to meet you and all..."). Their apparent indifference towards each other was so transparent it made their heads spin.

Their meeting was a celebration. It was a festival of youth. And desire. And deliverance. And cheap beer. But it was also a way of marking Neil's new job: cataloguing the contents of that old church and trapping its tower on paper before they tore it down to make room for an even taller tower. Huzzah for progress! It must have been quite a coup, Judith observed, for an English major to nab a job as a historian. And Neil had to agree. His other books were largely ignored. But now he was finally getting his due. Perhaps the church board had seen something in him that, until now, had remained dormant. Ambition? Talent? Why had no one nurtured it before?

They had so much in common. ("Red wine?" "Of course." "You like cheese too?" "Glorious!") When the waitress came to take their order, it took them five minutes to notice she was even there ("My goodness! Just like in the movies!" "Yeah, right, do you live alone?"). And while Judith laughed loudly at Neil's anecdotes, he emphatically praised her decision to drop journalism in order to focus on more worthwhile pursuits. Neil, never one for details, could not remember what Judith's new pursuits were, nor could he remember her last name, or whether he had even asked her, but such was his love that it didn't matter.

"It was destroying me creatively," she told him.

"No doubt," he replied, understanding exactly how she felt. "There was a time I was faced with a similar divergence in my path…"

And when the bars closed at two, they took a walk down by the lake, hardly touching. Scarcely a solitary house or man had been visible along the whole dreary distance of open lakeshore they were traversing; and now the landscape to their observation was enlivened by the quiet appearance of the planet Jupiter, momentarily gleaming in more intense brilliance in front of them, and by Sirius shedding its slobbery rays by Jupiter's side. The only lights apparent on earth were some spots of dull red, glowing here and there upon the distant overpasses, which, as Neil gratuitously remarked to her, were the smouldering fires of other burgeoning romances. And Judith felt electrified; a new world was opening up for her. Incredible! At the marina, looking back over the City, his eyes watering with nostalgia, he spoke to her of coincidence. It was amazing: without the skyscrapers and the yachts, the airplanes, the strip clubs, and the baseball stadium, it would be just like home.

"Just the duck?"

"Yes, the duck! That's exactly it." (She understood him!) "And the smell of slightly fetid water, of course."

"I think I love you," she said.

Oh, yes!

Then the rain began to fall. Wet hair. Beads on Judith's suede jacket. Nothing could dampen their moods, though. Like creative accountants, they present-ed each other with the briefs of their lives, mentally recording the debits and credits of the other for future analysis. They examined their date books, scheduled each other as much as possible into the coming year.

"And if you're not busy later, I thought we might, you know..."

"Oh, yes!"

Ah, wedding bells! How would it come to be? An elopement aboard a luxury cruise, of course. Like something out of *Love Boat*, but more fantastic. The Captain would be portly, and the stars would board the sky like pirates, hoarding the light in their pointed gullets until the night was as dark and pasty as Neil's tongue. The sprinkled flower petals would sprout flippered roots as they embraced the ground. And afterward, with the humidity settling to a more comfortable level and the sky opening to another coastal sunrise, they would throw a party, a celebration to usher in a new age of happiness, all their friends likewise ushered, by minibus, to a secret location, the road subsequently closed off, flashing mirrors at the hovering choppers, snapping the long arm of the press.

But back to the real world, which was wonderful enough when you thought about it. They kissed chastely beneath one of the Victorian lamps that blemished her street, and the teasing anticipation of sexual encounter, mixed with the teasing hand (hers) on a clenched buttock (also hers, much later, when she was alone), was enough to drive her mad with passion. Judith spun through the front door of her apartment, pirouetted, doffed her entirely inadequate wardrobe (her spirit was too free to be restrained by anything but love), and waltzed naked with the lanky hat rack beside the umbrella holder in her entryway. She soaked his photograph (showing off beside the seventeen-foot shark he landed on a trip with some college buddies from his undergraduate degree [the practical jokers Brandenberg and Bloom, along with Ferston, Mallow, and Mundus], his flesh tanned and wind-blown, taken by Marsh, who had captured himself in the reflection off Neil's Oakleys, Bloom yanking his shorts down around his ankles) in pouty kisses. And she leaned back against the door and tried to embrace her entire apartment, drawing all existence into the sweet hollowness she felt in her chest cavity, between her heart and her soul, before pulling the phone across the floor to her by its cord, her hand just then beginning to tease, imagining Neil's burgeoning lips on her hungry nipples, the tips of his calloused fingers grazing as he encircled her waist with his hands, she discovering all his hidden scars, every crevice, and nursing them with her tongue...

A voice on the other end: "Hello?"

"Oh, Burke, something absolutely wonderful has happened!"

XI. 'Her father did fume'

HOW COULD SHE know that, lurking in the darkness, huddled near her fireplace like a modern-day Zeus, was Tragedy, a black-bearded messenger who hated most of his children, but hated Judith least of all, and refused to lose her to some pencil-neck historian who didn't know his pen from his pecker. He had parked across the street from them at the bar, had spied on them from above and even killed the duck they had seen down by the marina. Neil would find it strung up outside his own home, neck broken, and fail to see it as significant ("Is a boy from the marshes not wanted in the City?" he wondered naïvely) until too late.

Because, even then, Tragedy was moving against them. "There's this thing he does with his eyes," Judith was telling Burke, twisting the cord around her left breast, "like he's trying to control my actions with his mind or some-thing, and it's sexy as— Holy shit!"—the cord went taut; there was a groan—"Where the fuck did you come from?" And something came wriggling out of the shadow like a gray snake, large as a bear yet glittering like wet leather.

Eyes black and gleaming. And a v-shaped mouth with rim-less lips that seemed to quiver and pulsate before the toothy hatch fell earthward and a long panting tongue lolled out. Her father's dog, with paws like roadblocks and a jaw like rolling logs. And the destructive wag of her sledgehammer tail took out most of her wall fixtures as she loped down the hallway. Tragedy, brown as autumn as to skin, white as winter as to clothes, came shambling after from the shadows, stubbing his toe on the fallen hat rack ("Geezus Kriiist!"); snatching the phone she held crotched between chin and shoulder blade; treating her more abruptly than she liked.

"I forbid you to see that boy again."

"What the fuck?!"

"You heard me."

And suddenly she was swept away by her estranged father to a distant land she had only dreamed of visiting.

"Judith?" Burke's voice called from the dangling receiver, desperate. "What's going on? Is there someone there with you?!"

Who could blame her for neglecting to call or write? Neil, dutiful to the chase if not to Judith specifically, called every second day, left a boiling pot of messages on her voice mail ("Hey, just called because I heard about another really cool show tonight... you must be away or something..."), but Judith was too mesmerized by her own pleasure—this storybook land of her father's, plunked somewhere between Egypt and Indonesia—to be concerned with regular external correspondence. Every morning her bedroom was full of flowers, with colours and shapes she had never seen before, stems and petals like models of atoms, capitulum structures like menorahs, or compound monochasiums, with flowers emerging from flowers emerging from flowers. Somewhere, she knew, there was a boy who loved her, but she was having such a lovely time, was learning so much. She had to learn to think more about herself.

Neil, who could think of little else, threw himself into his work, rebuilding the fantastic church tower word by word. He read other tower descriptions, from Babel to Babylon (he had no attention span for encyclopedias), but they all followed a formula, changing names while retaining the same basic structure. It was as if all towers were essentially the same. Neil, whose interest in the unique extended even beyond the prospects of scholarly recognition, revolted. He decided one should never describe a tower unless one could make it the only one of its kind in the world, which he would do through exhaustive enumeration. Not a tower like a well-formed sentence that runs on for pages, splashing like a duck in its own watery prose; or a concrete poem, many meanings in an eyeblink; but a tower like a phone book, or a stock inventory at a lumberyard, or an alphabet. A meaning, a definition, an essence. Found in the account of its elements. The bells, solid rejoicing and clangour, to be moved to the new structure. The windows, chorusing stained glass, to be sold to that Texan woman who had been in the news so much recently because of her alleged relationship with the scientist who had come to be known all over the world—alternately—as both Father Time and the Town Crock ("*Inte Klok?*" ran the punnish headline in more than one Swedish newspaper). To be replaced (note: must speak to Booting). Some old organ pipes. A cracked clay nativity scene. It would be the monument she would see and realize she still loved him, would return to him while he was sleeping and plant kisses all over him—

"This isn't some goddamn fairy tale," Marsh admonished him. "With dragons and architects and large, opulent bedrooms filled with flowers and jewels and peas. Towers don't attract princesses the way they used to. And why would she be impressed by a stupid collection of words as dead as stone? It's just a tower made of words. A descriptive paragraph without action. Don't you see she's not coming back?"

Yes. No. But how could he give up? He was pretty sure he loved her. And even though he hadn't come right out and said it like she had, he was fairly sure she knew. Meanwhile, *The Tower*. Would she see it, wherever she was, and understand?

Fuck it, Marsh was right. Besides, with his new interest in towers, and truth, and whatever else he could find to fill his day, Neil no longer had time for love. After a few weeks of unreturned phone calls (Burke kept pestering him about some sort of kidnapping, but he wasn't about to fall for that), he gave up on her, and cataloguing became his new obsession. His apartment on campus was near the garbage chute, and he began to keep a careful record of his neighbours' refuse habits. He took note of the return dates on random library books (a project that was soon abandoned because of its futility). Everything was broken down into lists and particulars, even his fiction, which became collections of words, testaments to the English language without a plot to speak of, nor characters, nor setting. His tidal prose of ebb and flow sentences was dropped for insects on cracked mallard eggs, dust lines on computer screens, and useless tacks stuck in useless walls. He began searching for a word that would include every letter of the alphabet, an *über*-word, which, if a child could be taught to learn that one word, he or she would immediately understand all of language. At least languages using the same alphabet system.

Neil began to picture himself as a visionary, and as such, he stopped shaving, let his hair grow out. One of the projects he assigned his third year class (were his freshmen ready for this sort of thing? he wondered) was to make lists of all the words used in the novel they were reading, then to analyze their findings in a concordance of sorts, listing everything by frequency first, and then alphabetically. He frequented readings, eschewing his normal prose for his new calling, spewing selective randomness like the first word of every page in Hardy's *A Pair of Blue Eyes*, or the page numbers of every mention of snow in Shelley's *Frankenstein*. He even stood up once in the middle of a crowded bar, shushed them all, and recited from his own concordance of his students' concordances, regressing this time from infrequency to frequency. The applause, after an unspecific amount of stunned silence, was sincere although timid. He envisioned himself as the last great flowering of English literature of the 20th century, and began cataloguing everything about himself for the reference of future generations:

July 1-, 200-

Food eaten: coffee, three eggs with toast, chocolate, more coffee, canned tuna, toast, a few beers, twelve cigarettes, a bottle of scotch, cookies, another cigarette...

Books read: *The Gothic Church Towers of England*, by Steve Smith; *Daughter of Hassan*, by Janet Dailey; *How to Talk Well*, by James F. Bender; the best-selling *Troubles with Tiplers: A History of Failed Time Travel*, by Dr. Ymer Framtiden, published posthumously; an old screenplay by William Faulkner in his younger days; several travel brochures; *Vogue Magazine*; *Boobs Magazine*.

Phone messages: none.

Work accomplished: one hundred pages, all handwritten, collected in a pile of yellow loose-leaf, *BOY MEETS GIRL* scrawled—almost illegibly in the final twenty or so—on every one.

XII. A father/daughter chat

TRAGEDY WAS FROM Away, born and raised on a mountain taller than any human-made structure. Not from the coastland of Neil's youth, where they romanticized lighthouses, nor from the City where the tower was an inescapable concrete symbol that caused everyone to feel smaller. The only towers he knew were ones of war. Or prisons. Or occasionally, as upon meeting Judith's mother Austral, he was reminded of his own cock, a whopper if ever there was one. Princesses were for prodding. Architects for building simple, practical housing. The hero, if he were worth his weight in anything, would stand in an open field surrounded by armed villains and never flinch, would hunt down what he wanted with only his trusty steed and perhaps a disposable sidekick. And writing?

"For pansies."

"Oh, Daddy, you'll never understand."

"Understand what? You're hot in the pants for someone who'd rather write about life than live it. What's not to understand?"

But Neil wasn't just another infatuation, nor was he idle; he was the stuff of heroes: a noble brow, hair like a choir boy, a dark yet respected lineage (his great-great-grandfather had once been the mayor, involved in a huge insurance scam—unproven—that left most of the river-side in ashes), made of velvet and steel. "Makes me feel like I'm melting," she once confessed to Burke. He was not, as many of her other boyfriends had been, the poor character who "mourned Romance," knew he was "born too late," told "uninteresting anecdotes," and sadly "kept on drinking." This was the one.

Tragedy did not believe it. "What we proclaim as the discovered factual love can be challenged as the questionable love we ourselves have painted."

"Have you been taking university courses?"

"Do you want a fat lip?"

"What about Mom? Was she just a figment of your imagination?"

"A passing fling."

"Mom?!"

"She got fat!" Tragedy protested. "Am I not human?"

"But how?" she asked him. "Didn't you want...? Don't you...? I mean, isn't it important...?"

"I can separate myself from love," Tragedy told her. "For me, it's a thing apart. But for you, Judy, it's your whole existence."

She felt faint. The moon attacked the balcony, set fire to the ivy, burned her eyes; and the Arabian sky, like the camels it sheltered, spit a star at the moon, which captured both their attentions, specifically Judith's. She wanted Neil, needed him.

"I wish... oh, I wish that..."

"If wishes were whores," Tragedy replied, "maybe then we'd all ride."

Tragedy and Austral

XIII. A creation myth, a destruction myth

JUST WHEN JUDITH thought she had banished Tragedy from her life forever, there he was, sitting on her kitchen floor reading her diary.

"What? No hug?"

"Fuck that shit..." She hadn't seen her father in years, not since the day he'd shown up at her sweet sixteen slumber party and tried to sleep with all of her friends, disguising himself as a shower of gold, a swan, Shaun Cassidy, a plate of fudge, a frozen brassiere, a brush handle, and ("Haven't you ever, you know, wondered?") one of the other girls. His only success: with young Litta, Judith's friend since first grade, who found his feathers strangely soothing. And here was the swan, hmmm, slipping her the pointiest, driest little tongue she'd ever had, and biting her as well, only much nicer, mmm-hmmm, like hair clips set against her skin, or the pinch of last year's swimsuit, pecking at her every joint and crevice. *Not even fairy tales were like this*, she was thinking when Judith's father goosed her right through her flannel. She swallowed her gum. "Are there two of you in there?" she wondered. And hitching the hem of her nightgown around her rib cage, pressing her bony hips against his webberied feet and ticklish underside, yanking the feathers from his back...

"Hey! Quit it, kid!"

Mmm-hmmm...

It was the honking that woke the rest of them.

"Mom!"

Judith's mother, Austral, was the First Nations French Canadian who had swum nearly every channel in the civilized world, competing for France in the 1960 Olympics because her home country did not recognize her unorthodox swimming style and felt she would be disqualified. She was. In the end, even the Japanese judge—with dreams of pearl-fishers capturing every single swimming gold in Tokyo—had to admit you can't swim the entire four-hundred-metre freestyle underwater. The American von Saltza received the laurels in her stead, and became a household name, as would Galina Prozumenschikova in her native Russia when the Olympics finally did hit Japan. It was Dawn Fraser from Australia who became everyone's darling in Rome, though, capturing the gold in the one-hundred-metre freestyle for the second of three consecutive Summer Games.

But the disqualification was hardly the turning point in the life of the young Métis. Not when you consider it was also the day Tragedy first approached her, in the shape of a bull, in the swim meet hot tub, as she was waiting for the decision to come down about her disqualification. An official protest had been launched by the Americans. Their weak arguments amounted to metaphor ("You can't fly in the one-hundred-metre dash, can you?") and hyperbole ("Next thing you know they'll be using submarines..."). But things still didn't look good. And as everyone's attention was locked on the pixel dot scoreboard, Austral's eyes went wide, with frantically swirling pockets of air coalescing into an upright bull before her, fast and spurious. Mesmerized, she forgot about the thousands of people in the swim hall, the millions watching at home, pulled aside the crotch of her regulation swimsuit and mouthed a prayer that it wouldn't hurt going in.

There was an audible click as the jaws of 128 million viewers flopped open (the entire world-wide audience for the most anticipated event of the 1960 games), when young Austral pulled herself from the pool-side tub, and her waist at least six or seven inches larger (driven straight to her third term by Tragedy's hormonal virility and bullish dong). It also shot her finally into the puberty that constant training and anorexia had held at bay for so long. And when the first orgasm racked her body ("No, thank you!" she squeaked to her coach at the edge of the tub, biting down hard on the towel he offered her. "I think I'll just stay in here a moment longer..."), she mistook that feeling for love. Lucky girl. The hard part was pushing out Judith a few months later, a little mewling brat with some kind of shiny substance covering most of her body. The doctors claimed it was a caul, said it would prevent her from developing properly, and removed it despite Tragedy's protests about natural defenses and image.

"A caul?!" Tragedy shouted. "Over her entire body?! Are you mad?" He tried to save her, even managed to smash through the protective barrier around the operating room, but the medical crew overwhelmed him with sheer numbers. With eleven nurses striding his chest—not a totally unpleasant experience, all said and done—he was forced to watch as they cut the second skin from his daughter. It would be cleaner, they said. Made for fewer complications. Definitely more attractive. Judith cried, but from pain more than from loss. Judith's mother said nothing, not that her protests would have done any better than her husband's.

Of course, by that time, Austral had already been stripped of her medals, and her words held little sway over the general public, let alone some imaginationless doctors. The young swimmer had captured the hearts of so many sportscasters when she first stepped onto the starting blocks, limbs like a newborn colt, nubs like swollen eyes. When she hit the wall seconds before any of her competitors, her Canadian homeland, which had refused to let her swim in the first place, rejoiced in her victory. In an unprecedented move by the government to dictate all television programming, not just the CBC, they forced every station to broadcast her victory speech. In French even! And when she asked for it ("What did she say? What did she say?" demanded the Prime Minister), the government passed a motion to increase funding to the national swim team.

When her laurels were removed, everything changed. Only in France—where they were all so revolutionary—was she still revered. Back home in Canada, the commercial she'd done for eggs never made it to television. People pointed at her skin, dark because of her Native mother, and commented about the untrustworthiness of immigrants. She fell from grace, and then completely from the public eye. Her abs and hips, still coated with the extra fat of her pregnancy, remained that way, began to swell with despair and chocolate cake. She never did get back into shape, and the more bloated she became, the less she interested the French.

"A real piece of ass, she was," Tragedy sighed. "Too bad she went to pot like that..."

Tragedy and Austral were the initial proud parents, rushing out to buy clunky new strollers, designer bibs, water wings ("Can't start too early..."), showing up at more family get-togethers, waking her up just to show the neighbours, or to amuse themselves. But that lasted maybe a month. After the early novelty wore off ("Aw, Geezus... This is a new tie! What are you feeding her? Diuretics?!"), the camera got hoofed into the corner with all the other discarded appliances of their short relationship together (the blender, the juicer, the electric knife), the re-gift pile from their shotgun wedding. Tragedy cut his paternal leave short. And little Judith—unable to even roll over because of those damn water wings, her pudgy little arms thrusting and retracting, pausing, kicking, cackling, sneezing, thrusting again—Judith was relegated to one spot on the kitchen floor directly in front of the fridge, forced to amuse herself with a magnetic poetry kit (she'd ingested the entire "The Waste Land" before they discovered what was going on and rushed her to the pediatric wing) while her mother stuffed herself with potato chips and fudge, tubes of chocolate chip cookie dough, gradually displacing more and more water from their Olympic-sized indoor pool. Judith wore those wings for more than ten years, until they popped, and never did learn to swim ("Mommy can't teach you now, Judy. She's waiting for the oven timer to go off..."), requiring them around water for the rest of her life.

Of course, Austral's memories required no visual documentation, puking every morning for three months, refitting her wedding dress over and over and over, and then having to go most of it alone because Tragedy suddenly became busy at work. There was some argument about what to name their darling child ("I was thinking of naming her after my Great Aunt Alice..."), but they eventually settled on Judith ("Alice? What are you talking about Alice? You want kids to make fun of her? *Dass ist Alles?!*") because Tragedy threw a fit at the supermarket, and it was easier to give in than to stand there all day.

And things just got worse from there. Who knew a kid could be so much work? Changing, watching, entertaining, feeding. Would her chlorined nipples do more damage than good? Her main problem was that her own life seemed so confused, and she despaired of ever being able to influence a life in a positive direction. She knew nothing of nurturing, consoling, the teaching of morals and fair play, not to mention proper technique, how to get the most loft and dive out of your butterfly, or how to measure length in breaths of air. The kid had a good set of lungs on her; that was for sure. And her kick seemed fine. But such tiny feet. So Austral watched baby Judith from the safety of the pool, her eyes surfing each billowing eddy of water and doubt, spouting like a whale ("Stop crying, baby... please, stop crying..."), wondering how she'd gotten into this mess all by herself. The only thing Tragedy contributed to Judith's upbringing was his foot, bringing it down on several occasions, most notably when Austral decided to try another comeback ("No kid of mine is going to grow up without a mother..."), and when Judith wanted to join Little League ("What, Aussie? You want her to grow up a dyke?").

Naturally, as soon as his little girl ripened into a teenager, Tragedy started showing interest again, volunteering to drive Judith and her friends to gymnastics, chaperoning school dances. What was the name of her friend with the quaint little miniskirt? My, my, that Litta was really developing into a fine young woman! Tragedy cut back on his office hours so they could "get in some quality time," going into semi-retirement, puttering around the house without a shirt, often joining Judy and her friends by the pool. But Judith was young, at an age where she was embarrassed by her parents ("Like, is that your *dad* lifting weights in the backyard?"), concerned about her popularity in the eyes of her fellow teens. She wanted to be more independent, to hang out with people who smoked even if she never would. When Tragedy suggested he might give them a lift to the movies ("You girls want a ride?"), Judith protested ("Mom!"), insisting she was old enough to have responsibility for the goddamn fucking car for one fucking night, and he really was too old to be looking at young girls that way, especially since he was married and all, which hurt him so visibly that she apologized and gave him a hug.

"What? I can't take my daughter out sometime?"

But Tragedy could be so conniving, deceitful ("Hoo yah!"). He tried to pull some of that tired, old, shape-shifting shit again, coming to one of her friends as a bicycle seat, to another as a frozen hot dog. And after Judith's sweet sixteen slumber party ("What are you talking about? We don't have a pet swan!"), Litta wanted to stay over every night. After Tragedy, she never slept with another boy again. In fact, she became a nun, believing she was still a virgin the rest of her life, and without sin, because it didn't count with birds, right?

God forbid, with all his screwing going on, Judith should even have a boyfriend. Or a date! At seven, if her father caught her chasing boys around the playground, he took the little Casanova aside and asked him which sandwich he'd rather have for lunch: peanut butter or knuckle? Or they were chased off by her younger brothers, Freddie and Flossie, the hunchbacked twins, named by Judith in her youth, with their clumsy gaits and hapless stutters ("B-buzz off, c-c-creep!" "If you kn-know what's g-g-good for you..."). By the time she was a teenager, everyone knew to steer well clear of her. And when she turned to her mother for support, Austral was too involved with her comeback to lend a hand. So she had no other recourse but to conduct her affairs in secret, rebelling as only one of Tragedy's progeny could, seducing various members of the big Greek's staff. To her French tutor, she revealed her true nature on an unchaperoned field trip (*"Aïe, aïe, petite fille fatale..."*), losing her *cerise* while riding him like a *cheval*. The brawny Scottish stablehand was calloused up to his elbows, and gripped her roughly from behind.

"Hey, Judy, know how I convinced your mother to go to bed with me?"

"You raped her!"

"Kids today... You have no respect for your elders..." Judith wanted to make her own worlds, something to call her own, instead of sneaking off with her father's estate as Tragedy had done to his father, popping emetics into the old man's drinks until it became impossible for the codger to run his companies properly, what with all those trips to the can ("...must have been something I ate, urp!... maybe the milk was, whoa!... bad after all..."). Tragedy, the youngest of all his siblings, was "chosen"— after long, drawn-out legal battles, the big Greek snorting and huffing as each decision was brought down in his favour ("Hoo yah!")—to lead the company into a new era, a new age of prosperity and growth. And his father was retired to a home, with an elaborate drainage system attached to a trough hanging from his wattled chin. A scale was designed to measure how much fluid he was losing each hour, replaced by IV ("Add haaaaaaafff a bottle of ipecac..."), a machine that made effective mobility nigh impossible.

"But he's well cared for, Judy," Tragedy was fond of saying. "Nurses with hands like that don't come cheap."

And Austral? She similarly disappeared from Judith's life after the comeback attempt in 1964. She was still a bit of a celebrity in Japan, the mother of a whole new sport there, but no one would have recognized her any more, even had she qualified for an Olympic berth. "Fat chance!" Tragedy bellowed, remembering Austral's rumpent waddle, and the hushed whispers as she mounted the second blocks. The gun was like a shot to her head and she hit the water like a wounded ostrich, the slap of her own fat against the pool loud enough to miss-start a track and field event in the nearby stadium. The competitors on either side of her were carried into the next lanes by her watery purls (including a number of medal hopefuls; the newspaper headline: *Undines Undone!*), and it was the swimmer in lane eight, a relative unknown named Marion Lay, only slightly ruffled by the aquatic ripples, who qualified for the national team, ultimately losing in the finals with a fifth place finish. (She would return again in 1968, improving her time by almost two seconds, on that occasion placing fourth). Austral, humiliated by her failure to regain the upper echelon of swimming's élite, and with last year's swimsuit biting into her potato-fed thighs, slipped out the back door of the showers, never to be seen again.

Rather than stay with her father, Judith ran away from home, travelled the world, and met up with a Dutch dye magnate named Venn. As she told Burke, it was the first time anyone had ever treated her like an equal, and they shared everything, including his intense fear of white, they were so close. But that's all she tended to disclose. And it was Booting who filled Burke in on the rest, with bits and pieces she disclosed during their body painting sessions. Venn obviously knew a good marketing scheme when he saw it, and he used her repeatedly as a flashy display board for his new colours of the season. Her calendar was on the wall of every interior designer in the world.

Booting also told him how Venn used her in numerous schemes to overthrow every other reddleman in the dye cartel: "So there she was, naked as a fucking goddess, her body turned red like a clay fertility statue by Venn's dye #36, butt-cheeks clenched around the tiny microphone he had supplied her so he could eavesdrop on everything. Giles Menzies, the self-proclaimed North American Kingpin of Pigments, slowly lowered his eyedropper when she stepped through the drapes, mistakenly blending two potentially volatile colours. There was a small explosion, and a few of the documents on his desk (contracts, recipes, debts of honour...) gathered the flame to them like moths. But with a pair of blue eyes like a whore's fucking pregnancy test, Judith made Menzies and his entire entourage oblivious to everything but her. Menzies had never seen a shade of brazilin-magenta so radiant before, particularly on a pair of boobies like that. And confronted with those crimson cantaloupes of hers, who could move? Venn slipped in completely unnoticed, rerouted all the pipes in the plant, and transformed the most resplendent gentian violets, annattos, and siennas into a gray-brown sludge that would have made fake mahogany panelling look even shittier."

Venn's personal stock skyrocketed. They bought a mansion on the coast where they might breathe the ocean. The fresh air would definitely do Venn's poor lungs some good, what with the bronchitis from all those fumes he worked in every day. It seemed as though everything was finally going Judith's way. This was the life she had dreamed of for so long...

Only, the dream soon turned into a nightmare. Poor Venn could see the potential for espionage in Judith but could not see his own end looming behind him like an arctic wasteland (his worst nightmare, nothing but colourless ice and snow). The Menzies clan never forgot what he had done to them. And they staked him out for several weeks before he could be taken alone, then blew the fucker up.

Of course, Venn was not alone when the Menzies boys kicked in the door, four against one, pinned him to the floor, punched IVs into his arms, legs, neck, and ass, catheters that pumped his body so full of his own dyes that he bloated up to nearly twice his normal size, his pores leaking magenta, his ears, cadmium; when they strung him up, his insides already ruptured by colour overdose, his veins standing out in maps of red and blue tracks, a huge piñata of flesh and dye; and when Giles Menzies himself fired the shot, painting the office in early Byzantine swaths. Judith, her own body dipped in sienna, a little umber, a touch of cutch, and a sprinkle of tannin, remained still against the wood paneling of Venn's office, somewhere between the sample shelf and the bar—who will ever know, the dye job was so good!—and waited until the top half of his body stopped spinning before unhooking the remains from the ceiling. Without any other choices, she picked up the phone and called Tragedy, who answered on the first ring.

Just as he always seemed to show up whenever she'd meet someone new, and was there to comfort her when each of them met with some horrible, accidental fate.

For her, just seeing him—particularly right now, in the City—was a sign of bad luck.

For Tragedy, these reunions were like new beginnings. Now they could be the family he'd always dreamed of: "You know, like in... that story... with the father... and the daughter..."

"*You* ran out on me *too*!"

"What?! Are you gonna call me on that *now*? Who's this Neil patsy I keep reading about?"

Neil and The Tower

XIV. 'Where heaves the turf in many a mould'ring heap.'

ALL JUDITH WANTED was a normal family life, not the Greek sporting arena into which she spurted, her mother dropping her nine-month load during training ("Just feeling a little queasy," Austral explained when she returned from the changing room. "I'm fine now..."), and Tragedy, saddled with the new responsibility of a wife and child, fathering umpteen more (from the moment they were born, wedged in their mother's *la-la* on their way out, Freddie and Flossie perched grotesquely over their dear, dear sister). So, when Tragedy tried to force his way into her life again, she warned him to back off, to stay away from Neil (not to mention Anne-Sophie and Booting), and the big Greek merely shrugged and pulled on his cardigan:

"Geezus, Judy?! Is that how you want me to spend my retirement? I'm too old to party with you and your friends any more..."

"So you don't hate Neil?"

"Neil who?"

"Oh, Daddy!"

At least that was the way Burke imagined it happening. How else, when he eventually ran into her on campus after her date with Neil, could he reconcile her present immediacy with the story he'd already created for her? And his only comfort, as he gradually managed to block out her claims to chemistry, was that happiness was the most unstable of elements. How could it ever work? Judith had dreams—night and day thoughts like the opening of yellowy eyes—of she and Neil in blissful cohabitation by the ocean, washing the dog, the planting of commemorative saplings, buying cars that were not too run-down. And Neil? The bastard. Neil dreamed he was in a tower (a very natural dream for a head filled like his with the sexually morbid, the sectionally mortared: his work on the church), and on the lowermost banister of a great staircase, he saw a gigantic hand in armour (something silvery, metallic; not really so huge, but definitely scary), clutching between finger and finger and finger and finger and thumb: a book, with his name written all over it.

"Nice to know that you think of me sometimes..."

"Fuck, Jude, it was a dream!"

Between her own thumb and forefinger, a tiny violin...

And they were already headed in opposite directions by that point, their relationship caught up in conflictual obsessions and ideologies, their home no longer a castle. "When are you going to do the dishes?" he asked. "When are you going to shut your hole?" she replied. The incongruity of their dreams was just the final straw. He'd become aloof. His endearingly quick temper and artistic assuredness had been replaced by a demonic quality as well as a Faustian egotism, already so far gone, his body dreadfully emaciated by fatigue and inspiration. For someone who was supposedly so attuned to details, he couldn't seem to remember simple things like scheduling ("Why do we have to meet your friends so early, again?"), people's names ("For fuck's sake, Neil, his name is Tragedy, not 'that asshole'..."), or even her birthday. He was so wrapped up in his work, they went weeks without seeing each other, at least nothing—"Do you need anything at the store?"—on a meaningful level.

The world was no longer large enough for him, no longer real enough, mere existence no longer an acceptable alternative. Everything had become a mush of doing and thinking and moving and writing, a porridging sludge of inertia and co-adductive activity. For Neil, the dream was a new understanding of his situation, the final clue he'd been searching for, the inspiration to finish what would be the most oft-discussed book of his time; and from that day literature—and particularly prose, in the most comprehensive sense of the term—became nearly his sole occupation. The ancient writers had promised great impossibilities, striving to elucidate human nature and behaviour through the exhaustive reiteration of theme, motive, stock scenes, and dialogical traits. Even when they were describing metaphorical monsters or dystopic near-futures, they promised to explain why things were the way they were. Complete understanding. But they had performed nothing. Throughout literature, the same boring thoughts continued to occur, again and again, in every possible variety of phrase. Neil, on the other hand, would succeed where they had failed, by ignoring the wanky psycho-babble and exhaustive descriptions and concentrating instead on the nuts and bolts of it all, the screws rather than the screwing, recreating towers and thunderstorms and all humanity simply by duplicating only their most basic elements. A list of all possibilities. Just as the infinite string of numbers in Pi was supposed to contain every possible sequence and permutation.

And he spent most of his time behind the doors of the tower until "the novel" was finished, doing his best to destroy metaphor forever.

It was the winter. That endless kind of winter you only saw in horror novels and Canadian epics. It was also the winter when Judith left Neil because he failed to remember she was the most important thing in his life. She didn't understand him, thought he was some kind of monster because he didn't wash out the bathtub once a week, or he wasn't upset about the prospect of death, or he didn't send cards on appropriate occasions. The first time he told her he never apologized for anything ("I'm sure I had good reasons to do it in the first place; what good is it to keep second guessing yourself your whole life?"), she looked as though he had physically struck her. Judith wanted to spend more time with him, but to him, because of his obsessive lists, she was no more than an enumerated object. It confused him to set eyes upon her more than once a day. He worked on *The Tower* for days on end, collapsing narcoleptically at his desk, while going down the stairs, while going down on her, or in the shower.

"He comes and goes like a spirit," she told Burke. "No one can anticipate when or where."

Meanwhile, inspired by the dream, Neil continued to explore. It had only been a dream, certainly. But there were aspects that seemed so real, and surely enough, at the bottom of the tower's main stairwell, just as he was nearing the completion of his initial list, was a tiny trapdoor. A doorway to an entirely new book, expanding his simple list of every item in the old church tower to a list of every item in the entire City. Through the trapdoor: a tunnel. And another tunnel. And another. Until it became clear he was no longer anywhere near the tower, or even the graveyard next to it. What did it mean? At that point, he was still unsure. But on successive nights, after the full scope of the tunnels had dawned on him, he realized this was his opportunity to not only recreate a tower, but something much greater. Through the City's extensive sewer system, he was granted access to all their homes. And snaking through their walls and floors, spying on them through the knots and electrical outlets, he exposed all the secrets of their being. Their dreams. The things they were creating when no one was looking. Not through their actions, which he dismissed as nothing more than the predicates of existence, the possibilities of thought, but rather through their possessions and discards, the residue of creation, the trace from concept to obsession.

Their stuff.

And as his scope spread outward, *The Tower* continued to grow, became a communal confession, the timeless record of their private and public fetishes, a city's piece-by-piece deconstruction. Sure, there were the unfinished sweaters and rusting trombones, the meticulous lists of resolutions and other forgotten projects, these things that hinted at some purpose. But even that was probably reading too much into it, some internal desire we have to add drama to any situation. If he were a carpenter building a table, he would need wood. And screws. And the motivation of those same screws would be irrelevant, if not laughable. So why recreate existence any differently? Instead, his documentation, starting with the sewers, marked every trashy chicken carcass and mouldering Brie wheel; useless rusty old pot scrubbers; the monstrous, garbage-eating offspring of discarded pet goldfish and turtles; and it gradually grew to encompass every object in every home, down to each half-empty paint can and spare sink plug. The stuff this world was really built on. A gloriously complete glossary to be reordered and analyzed. Reshaped! He'd discovered the secret of creation, a second Babel disguised as a novel, reaching toward paradise on stacked *p*'s and *d*'s. He also began to believe he could remove any solid object like a word, rubbing it out without even the trace of eraser spoor. He just needed more things to list.

Exhausting the mysterious tunnels he'd inherited, he started to dig his own.

...which was when he found the bodies...

...and the book with his own name.

XV. A lovers' disagreement

HE'D BEEN SLEEPING in the church tower for weeks, sustaining himself at first on leftover bread and wine, then sneaking out at night to forage for supplies. That sacrament stuff could only last so long, you know. And although the locals feared him like the devil, particularly when he would abruptly materialize in their kitchens asking for sandwiches and Coke, they found it difficult to refuse his requests. He was so lonely, so lovely, so charismatic with that shock of black hair on his blue-pale face. His words were like timeless monoliths, dark and imposing. And when he looked at them straight in the eye, they knew they were his.

Every new addition to his list had been another nail in the coffin of his sanity: congested organ pipes, a stained glass depiction of the Crucifixion of Christ with a crowd surrounding a strange looking metallic cow, bats in the belfry, cats in the clerestory! But it was the bodies and the mysterious book that truly possessed him, what woke him from sleep, made him doubt his own pursuits. And yet... He found he couldn't stop. It was in his nature, his character. Lists were the altar on which he'd laid his worshipful pen. And the bodies of this mother and child—this skeletal Madonna and her emaciated offspring—were simply the last straw. Just as he had with everything else, he began dismantling them, examining each piece not as the connector for the two bones on either end of it, but singularly, without predetermined meaning or placement. And through these experiments he realized he could alter their shape into anything he dreamed: a man with legs for arms; little people constructed only from phalanges, carpals, and tarsals; a second head postulating from the posterior; or even a design for the perfect assembly line employee, without a head at all, but four lovely loosied arms to apply whipped cream to twice as many cakes, and twice as many cherries.

He even brought Judith and Marsh to see it.

"See here how the fingers seem so extended from the rest of the hand? Almost like they were flippers instead of hands? Perhaps a missing link from the time we were more aquatic? Some kind of ancient creature or demon kept here by the priests?"

And when she pointed out that this wasn't a Catholic church, it was Presbyterian, when she urged him to call the Chief Inspector, he grew irritable: "But this is Art, Jude! There's no place here for authority and rules!"

It was also how he realized he could put these discoveries to use on himself, which quickly became his one thought, his one conception, his one prime directive. A rebirth as someone else entirely! He was alive! And Marsh was there to capture the whole thing on film. As Neil's victorious eyes dwelled upon them with all their melancholy sweetness, Marsh blasted away with the Imacon 1 (an early prototype for the much-faster Imacon 600, itself able to walk away from ballistic research with six-hundred million pictures per second), snapping up footage of Neil's every twitch, each willful burst, every hand raised in animation. Unfortunately, the flash visibly irritated the writer, sent him into wild fits where he refused to continue the story of the bodies properly. When Marsh refused to let up, Neil punched a hole in the wall before leaving.

"He's afraid," Judith said. "Anyone can see it."

Afraid of what, though? Mediocrity? Failure? Commitment? Even before the novel came out, his agent had already created a substantial buzz. It was sure to be a success. How could anything be wrong?

But there was no way they could have known about the molemen Neil saw around every corner, an urban legend that seemed to be spreading throughout the City. They were under the streets, some people said, under the bed and in your hair, these little molemen with their hunched backs, mining helmets bearing futuristic lanterns, with their ability to collapse their skulls, their rumpy humps, and even their tails (yes, tails, they were so much wrath and vermin!), so that they could pass under your door, take away your children! They could fly, perhaps (that wasn't so unlikely, considering), walk through walls (although why would they have to, if the whole passing-under-doors thing were true), knew your thoughts before you had thunk them, could perform loathsome acts with diplomatic immunity. Even in the sewers they tracked him, these strange hunched beasts who snuffled and gurgled through the City's ass droppings, alerting him to their presence as their bubbly shoulders connected with the sewer's stone supports ("Fawk!" "Watch it, n-n-n-numbnuts!" "Screw you, d-d-dickwad!"). Each time he managed to escape by altering the text of his underground construction, this grammar-less architecture, throwing up decoy semi-columns or dangling from a partition until they gave up on him for the day. But they were getting closer. And so Neil showed up unexpectedly in Booting's apartment one night, fading into existence at the window, dripping with melted snow, his sentences crumbled, disjointed, like the vocabularies of polysyllabic infants. The glazier was the only one he could trust. The rest of them had too many aspirations. He had to protect the original manuscript, depositing the entire mess ("The ultimate secrets of Heaven and Earth!" he snarled between his inarticulate sturmurings) at Booting's feet.

"Before I depart, I will give them to you, they will prove the truth of my tale..."

"..."

Then, clearly, cryptically, Germanically: "*Was du ererbt von deinen Vätern hast, erwirb es, um es zu besitzen...*"

What you have inherited from your fathers, make it your own in order to possess it...

"Denn die Todten reiten währendzeiti..."

For the Dead travel through time...

"Evermore."

It crushed Judith to witness him drifting as he was, exhibiting signs of dyslexic motion and aural decomposition, forgetting to bend at the elbows and knees, thrashing his arms about madly as he walked, cracking his forehead against door frame peaks. She longed for the early days, when everything was still a metaphor for love, unnecessary to interpret. She wanted a boyfriend who was on the edge, not over it. She could see how far he'd fallen, could make out each dent in his sanity. But when she urged him to return to his other novel, to abandon this monstrous study of the bodies, the uncouth and inarticulate sounds that broke from him frightened her into silence again.

"Where did you hear about that?" he attacked her. She meant *The Assassins*. His first book, that was inspired by his own youth ("I was a beautiful boy at fifteen..."), and took the form of an adolescent detective/hitman/ethics agency, starring three mentally advanced teenagers (a Hegelian, a follower of Kant, and a pudgy one, but all essentially interchangeable) who had taken it upon themselves to free mankind from the tyranny of power usurped by kings and priests and parents. All with a little help from Angela Lansbury (a trope he planned to have recur in each successive volume). He knew she meant well. She was concerned about how his experiments with the bodies were affecting him. And she didn't even know about the book he'd found. But compared to his newest obsessions, it was nothing. And he snarled at her, rose sullenly, and spoke his only coherent line that night:

"To examine the causes of life, we must first have recourse to death."

Although Neil inhabited her apartment like moon-light, there were times like this that he seemed almost sane. He was cordial as they relived old times, like their first meeting ("I promised myself, you know, if I ever saw you again..."), or the time they'd had sex in her parents' basement and he had to turn all Tragedy's hunting pictures to face the wall. They discussed art, *Paradise Lost*, the latest jokes about Sweden's *Time Bandit* ("He lost his *tempor*! har, har, har!"), pressure-treated wood, the voluntary motion of vermicelli (night waned upon this talk, and waned some more before Neil took their leave). But the smoke from his cigar made it difficult to see his face, so Judith was unsure of his sincerity when he asked them for help. He insisted they leave the lights extinguished. He was concerned with poison, and refused to touch the dinner she had prepared. When he made his way to the bathroom ("Once you break the seal," he joked), he moved with the hinge-kneed gait of a wounded heron, as if he were, in reality, a clever group of midgets in costume. And on his return, Judith noticed the limp ("No,

Jude, don't get up..."), the hunched shuffle. His parts were no longer working together.

They cried. But he swore he was back. He loved her. And he wanted to make a stronger go of it. He wanted to get better. He even accepted Marsh's invitation to his art opening. Only he wasn't expecting to be the main subject matter, the "Turret Laureate" on freakish display, the progeny of the Imacon. With permission—no, encouragement—from Neil's obscenely overweight agent Giesler, Marsh had plastered every square inch of the gallery—there were even several hundred piled in the middle of the floor—with the complete process of Neil's maniacal grin, thousands of shots depicting every muscle and jaw, the feral retraction of his lips, the torrid nostril flare. Giesler though it might cause some more buzz. Sucking on cloves to disguise the stench of his sinus infection ("As a kid, I used to ram pencils up my nose. You know, to see how far they'd go..."), he showed up with some gorgeous physicist Marsh spent the evening trying to pick up. In return, Giesler burrowed into the corner with Marsh's girlfriend Isabella and a few of his best jokes, screwing up both his punchlines and his nerve: "Wanna know how to get fucked? Crawl up a chicken's ass and wait!" Neil was in the papers for weeks. Both Marsh and Giesler considered it a huge success.

For Neil, though, who was trying so hard to fight his inventorial addiction (to re-enter the world of man), it was all too much, this confrontation with the wretch he had created (sight tremendous and abhorred!). He wasn't sure who he was any more, was separating, falling apart, and Marsh's photos only multiplied this effect, accelerated it. Each day he returned to the gallery, he used Marsh's photos to study each step and stumble, every gesture, in fine detail, defining the breaks between flexions, working on each move separately, perfecting them. His movements became even less fluid, regressed until each part was a subtraction from the sum. And faced with such hideous divisions of himself, he lurched back to the tower, closed himself up entirely. He completely lost it, stepped out the tower's window, and headed up, up, up...

Below, with Marsh struggling with his camera strap, his flash lighting the sky like a vast sheet of fire ("C'mon, buddy! This is your re-birth, this is your anthem!"), Judith stood fixed, gazing intently upward. She could not be mistaken; Marsh's flash illuminated the object, and discovered its shape plainly to her: Neil, his groin pressed into the side of the tower, some fifty feet in the air, one hand gripping his fabled manuscript, ripped and darrowed and fey, the other fist ("My God, Neil, take hold of the bell screens!") shaking angrily at the crowd that had gathered below to witness his fall. Suddenly, the world she knew began to spin, and with each thunderous pop of the flash, Neil's form became apparent to her far along the adjacent buildings, from tower to tower, the clanging bells among leaps the live thunder.

HALF, THE SECOND

Anne-Sophie and Nästa

XVI. A star is born

ANNE-SOPHIE SORET was the consummate performer, her combinative parts made purely for Köchelic amplification and acoustic metronomy. Her parents—*she* was a failed singer herself; *he* just had strange ideas about procreation and an obsession with America—had been working on their little peeper for some time; scheduling their lovemaking sessions on the birthdays of famous composers and sopranos; playing Wagner records at full blast as Ginetta Soret rode her husband like a raging Valkyrie, in their tenement house on *Rue Bato* in Paris, the beating of their neighbour's broom against the ceiling a percussively steady contrast to the couple's jerky lead movements; and eating mostly beans and cabbage in hopes that the extra air from the foods would fill the child's lungs. They were intending to spring their little soprano as a surprise on the music world ("We didn't want anyone else to steal our ideas and beat us to the punch..."). However, by the time they were ready to release their invention, word of their experiments had reached the press, and on the way to the hospital, the

Sorets' taxi was struck from behind by the overeager paparazzi. Anne-Sophie's mother emitted a shriek unlike any she'd ever managed to hit before, a high F that blew out the cab windows, rendering the *chauffeur de taxi* unconscious. And right on beat (Louis "John" Soret was his wife's breathing coach, and he was not about to stop counting for a minor traffic incident), tiny Anne-Sophie entered the tone-deaf world, adding a near perfect harmony (even higher!) to her mother's screams of agony. It took John Soret only a few moments (he was likewise stunned by the piercing polyphony) to realize this was his daughter's own post-natal wail.

"*Un peu plat,* but not bad, *n'est-ce pas?*"

For the most part, Anne-Sophie's parents left her in the care of her German vocal coach, a harsh woman who forced her to practice on pieces like Mozart's *Popoli di Tessaglia* (for range) and Brünnhilde's immolation scene (for endurance). And this was mostly just to work the bugs out of her. There was no holding back the talent her parents had instilled in her. By the age of four, her prodigy was already known outside her local cathedral. At nine, she was invited to appear as Rosina in *The Barber of Seville.* And before she was even put on the pill, she could produce fordonic frequencies to shatter nearby crystal. On the day of her first period, when she spotted the rash of rusty blood after practice, she feared she had broken something inside her. By thirteen, she was performing to crowds numbering in the six figures without electronic amplification.

She was her parents' dream: a singing machine. But like all creations of beauty, she also revealed the potential for great destruction early on. Before she had learned to master her talents, using nothing but the hypersonic blow of her boundless pipes, she nearly caused premature deafness in a crowd of infant music students. And after a performance for the French National Assembly, when her lungs, diaphragm, and enlarged vocal chords were just reaching maturity, they were forced to replace an entire wall of the *Centre Georges Pompidou*. She was still selling out huge stadium performances, but she'd been made to feel embarrassed by her gift. So much so that, when she finally met the cellist Nästa, while she was supposed to be seeing Burke, she was afraid to let him that close to her. The first time they were intimate, he ventured to slip a few fingers inside her scarves, and she placed a restraining hand on his.

"I'm not normal. You're not going to bed with a real woman. But don't be disappointed, okay? Have you ever made love to a freak before?"

Had he?! He was on the hunt for them. Girls with beards, gills, tentacles, symmetric osteal ridges; covered in fur, scales, religious psychotactual tattoos. The only real difference between those other women and Anne-Sophie was that she couldn't speak perfect English. And, of course, Nästa saw more promise in the French chanteuse than he'd seen in any performer for years. She was the final element he needed for his anomalic circus;

all she needed was a little proper engineering.

Nästa knew the freak show business like no other. A physical anomalist visionary. And he picked up where the Soret's nanny had left off, reinforcing Anne-Sophie's gift using his own myological theories. He had special baby soothers manufactured at great expense, the nipple over a foot long and shaped from solid steel. For two to three hours a day, she was connected to a nemectronic electrical generator, each surge tensing, stretching, releasing, tearing, building. And in the City strip bars, he worked on her act, her cantilinear program, fine-tuning each crush and tremolo, every pitch and flexion. More than anything, he implanted in her a greater understanding of the stage, a showmanship on par with Lewis or Sellers.

It was Nästa who brought her to the big time, rescued her from performing arias for middle-class salesmen and their wives, and got her swallowing all sorts of things (bananas, frozen freeze pops, miniature baseball bats...) for the same salesmen, minus their wives, at a tavern near the docks. Hardly the beginning you'd expect for the future *Prima Down-ah*, but, hey, everyone has to start somewhere. And people did come to see her, partly because of the strippers (the neon outside flashed *Cold Beer! Hot Ladies!*), but also because the cellist was a master marketer. Posters with grotesquely exaggerated representations of Anne-Sophie were stapled to every telephone pole around, the eye-level pole rung bent and dripping with saliva. He hired a couple of hunchbacked twins ("W-w-when do we st-st-start?" "W-w-where's the st-st-st-star?") to bark announcements on the pier outside. And everyone who brought a flat metal disc to the show (1" in diameter and 1/16" thick, for sale in the foyer) was assured of having it embossed (a new trick she was working on: precision muscular flexion) with their name, the date, and their own crowned profile. Meanwhile, he was assembling a supporting cast the likes of which had never been seen together in one place: Peter Piltdown, a genuine cave man from the Australopithecine Age, trained to build small fires, a skill well beyond the normal brain capacity for a man from that period; Siamese triplets; a man who was only arms and legs, without a torso; a giant ape ("Where he comes from, he's a king, but for you..."); a boy-faced dog; and the geeks. Not just the regular caged-up geeks, either, but top-of-the-line glommers who ate glass, bugs, porcelain urinals, symbols of the communist regime, crow, their pride, their words! the stage! themselves! All he needed was the venue ("The geeks are excellent carpenters, so don't worry, they'll replace anything they eat..."), and a little financial backing ("Do you think carpenter geeks come cheap?"), and he would make Barnum look like a child making monsters out of pipe cleaners and pig heads. This was the real thing. These were real freaks.

"Not unique, but as different from us as possible, so when the prodding stick starts poking, the audience stands no chance of feeling it. It's not a show, or a fucking performance or something, it's an exhibit! Christ, anyone can learn how to *do* something! People want to see something that they could never *be*!" This was the future of art! Not creating or uncreating, or making or unmaking, but be-ing!

He had Anne-Sophie in major training: a strict diet of Creatin and carbs; running her through autocrash simulation equipment to build whiplash resistance; no-armed push-ups (elevating her body by driving her forehead into the floor); and a steady stream of progressively harder substances down the ol' fruit chute. Shattering crystal was a parlour trick. Even pulping timber with your tonsils became kid's stuff. If they wanted to keep the people coming for more, they needed to really wow them.

"Perhaps I may not make any money by this enterprise," he sheeped at the press conference for the new show, "but I assure you that if I knew I should not realize a farthing profit, I would yet ratify the engagement, so anxious am I that this area shall be graced by a lady whose vocal powers have never been approached by any other human being; and whose character is charity, simplicity, and goodness personified..."

At which he turned viciously on her, drew his pistol, and fired.

The tent was packed every night.

XVII. The physical anomalist's dream

FOR NÄSTA, THE show was the culmination of all his twisted dreams, the vision that had drawn him ever since losing his virginity to a nine-hundred-and-eleven-pound exhibit who had renamed herself as Ida Maitland. "Nästa, Nästa," the other boys screamed. "We are going to see Ida!" And he followed them all—"I'm coming!"— to the beachside shop. Not only was she grotesquely obese, a mythic sea monster with seaweed hair, barely able to move, crammed into a glass tank of water that seemed barely large enough to contain her, she also had the most beautiful pair of blue eyes, and a hoarse, two-fisted smoker's voice that she used to ask him to retrieve one of her cakes from the tiny Easy-Bake Oven she kept just to the side. The other boys danced around her, holding their arms out to the side and puffing out their cheeks. They mocked her peasant French accent. They watched as she was fed tubes of cookie dough from a diving board above her, not even bothering to remove the wrapper. But Nästa felt compassion. He felt turned on.

So much so that he snuck back later that night, slipped under the tent cover, and took to her spanscape like an Arctic explorer, plunging and resurfacing over and over in her pruny folds. After her last husband, she said, she could barely feel a thing. But when she shifted her weight, it rubbed him from all directions at once. And he came almost immediately.

The show was his ode to Ida. It marked the proliferation of Freak culture, a circus very much like the cinema. Within months they were clambering for it on Broadway, in London, Toronto, the City. For a while he considered franchising. But there was only one star. He'd tried to duplicate Anne-Sophie's talents by starting a new music school, with past winners of the Mr. Universe competition as vocal coaches. But they failed to produce anyone who could get past snapping twigs *or* high C. So Nästa contented himself with touring plans (just the major cities, to whet their appetites), appearances on the *Late Show*, *Oprah*, *Rosie O'Donnell*, *Larry Sanders*, and then a huge international marketing drive involving t-shirts, lunchboxes, biographies, and scarves, a CD of crystal-smashing frequencies, a special edition Barbie doll (*Press the button on her back, and her throat crushes Play-Doh lead pipes... Play-Doh lead pipe manufacturer sold separately...*), and a weekly television variety show featuring the moment's hottest pop stars with the best of the best in the world of side show freaks: an entire soccer team of Brazilian skiapodes, feet the size of parasols; the appalling Nino; and the shock of the century, an interview with an aging fascist monorchid, long-believed poisoned with cyanide and brained with his own 7.65 mm Walther pistol.

In the world of the Normals, Anne-Sophie Soret became a household name. To the Freaks, however, she was like a rallying point. It seemed to her that they had looked at her in a secret way. They tried to connect their eyes with hers as though to say, we know you. We are you!

And she was afraid.

XVIII. Another opera

NÄSTA'S GREAT-GREAT-Uncle Sol (the human calculator) had formed the first sideshow union in 1898. Sol, with a face reddened by moral indignation (and a heavy smooching session with his secret lover: the deliciously hirsute Miss Annie Jones), encouraged them to throw down the shackles of their keepers, Ballarneyum and his Bailiff, imposing a work stoppage until their demands were met. Demand #1: The performers wanted a say in how the shows were run. #2: They wanted more money. #3: They wanted respect. Sol convinced them that their worldwide numbers (he quickly summarized) were strong enough to be heard, so long as they stood together. But Bailey manifested at the meeting with a gang of toughs to dissuade them from any "ridiculous actions," and within five minutes the new union had voted unanimously to disband. That Barnum guy wasn't *so* bad, *really*, I mean he had given them something to do, and even if they had to fend for themselves after retirement, they had enough to eat right here and right now...

"Armless Wonder?" Uncle Sol confronted the union secretary who kept the minutes with his feet. At the moment of confrontation, he'd hid behind the Fat Lady. "More like the Gutless Wonder!"

It was Anne-Sophie, though, through her own self-imposed transformation, over a hundred years later (some glorified it as self-mutilation), who offered them renewed strength and pride. The weekly live broadcast of her *Howl Hour* made it hip to be a freak again, and perfectly normal people held parades to embrace their previously closeted differences. The real fanatics showed their zeal by cutting off ears, having their spines surgically bent, taping their fingers together until their hands gradually became useless fins (which would become an issue at the next Olympics, but that's another story). For others, the moderate and temporally stylish, they were satisfied with small shows of solidarity and support. Biting the heads off chickens was back in style. Young girls eased themselves into obscenely tight t-shirts with slogans like *Fairy Tail* and *Double Humper*. Opera was In. And strangely, piercings were Out, unless they were through the cheek, the mandible, or long blades driven straight through the stomach.

She was already such a public figure that her every move was covered in newspapers from the local *Tribune-Post* to Sweden's *Dagens Nyheter*. (The debate over physicist Ymer Framtiden's time travel discovery was moved to page two for one day.) But Nästa and Anne-Sophie had even bigger dreams, to bring real opera back to the masses, something by a new composer, to create a role that would be entirely her own, not simply part of a longer tradition. All these old stories retold and retold, shit, who wanted to hear about that mythic legendary crap? Why not something set in the future? "A *Star Trek* meets Mozart kind of thing." Now Nästa was flying. "Like that episode where they fight Liberace!"

Yes!

Unfortunately, aside from the sellout crowd on opening night, no one saw Anne-Sophie's performance of *The Eighty-Minute Hour*, something Nästa would never fully understand. Was it not filled with the prerequisite romantic setting? determinism? melodrama? melodic gymnastics? personal conflict? the expectation of cosmic cataclysm? Heck, they'd even dropped in a few chase scenes for the nosebleed section. Futuristic gadgets. And just a little T&A. The composer had rendered the lead female as "old enough to stand at once as sex-symbol and mother-figure," but Anne-Sophie's Glamis Fevertrees had been younged-down a bit, concentrating more on the sexy angle. Her wardrobe consisted mostly of duct tape, with pigtails and a cowboy hat. When she first took the stage, they had to pause five minutes until the applause petered out.

But that was the high point of the evening. Apparently, Nästa failed to properly gauge the public's interest in the foreign ingenue. At four of the opera's own hours (two hundred and forty minutes!), it was just too much for the average person to take. When Glamis and Jules de l'Isle Evens (a re-energized William Shatner) became stranded on what would later become Earth, an anachronistic Adam and Eve whose bodies would be buried and discovered millennia later (A-S: *From there the stages, difficult but placid, / That led us upwards to the human race, / Are now deterministically clear...*), the place began to clear. When Shatner intoned the romantic line, "We two are... alone. I beg of you, I... beg... of you," his words took on new meaning. The place was empty. The critics pronounced A-S's performance as lifeless, stiff, without emotion, like the clattering of nuts and bolts in a tin box. Only Booting, whose body was quickly giving up on him, would ever rave about the space opera. Strangely, Anne-Sophie's performance had given the crumbling glazier a renewed hope, when he misheard, and hence misquoted, the musical's closing lines, making them his own personal mantra:

"If a one-legged dreamer can save the world, surely another can win it..."

Of course, the executive producer of Anne-Sophie's television variety hit would have said her career was dead a long time before that. As it turned into more of a family-centred variety show, focusing more and more on the guests than on Soret's wondrous throat, *The Howl Hour* was losing its core audience. There was still a sizeable following of sideshow performers tuning in (at least the

Nielson freak demographic never missed an episode), but they purchased so little that could be advertised on television. They were not in possession of disposable income. When it came time to make the final cancellation decision, the executive producer let her know through a note couriered in a potted plant: *You were great*, it read. *Thanks a lot. You're through.*

XIX. 'A charming snap.'

NÄSTA FOLDED HIS copy of Jack Earle's *The Long Shadows* on the cast-iron table, lit another *Gauloise*.

"I will never give up on you."

And from that day forward, he brought her back to her more sexually intimate beginnings, although on a much grander scale than those strip club back rooms, introducing her to the world of mass pornography. Relying on kitsch appeal to sell a few extra copies, *Playboy* featured a spread entitled *Diva au Naturel*, "dressing her" in the roles of Brünnhilde (braids and helmet) and Elektra (an outfit more closely resembling Spiderman's nemesis Electro, with a head wreath fashioned out of neon yellow lightning bolts, matching belt and boots), as well as Minnelli's *Cabaret* bow tie, and a pair of ruby slippers. *Boobs Magazine* followed suit, minus any pretense (or arty costumes), substituting a loose plot structure involving a backstage tryst and the conductor's "baton." And the *pièce de résistance*: the French chanteuse was cast in the starring role of an elaborate, blue, sci-fi production of Strauss' *Salome*, renamed *Salope*, which culminated in a huge orgy scene, He-Rod (a superhero from another planet and dimension, with a huge penis he kept slung over his shoulder) promising her whatever she desired as he was stroked fiercely by her mother (He-Rod-Yes), and Anne-Sophie pleading to give head to Long John the Baptist (played by rising star Ian Dowd).

"Ah! Thou wouldst not suffer me to suck thy cock, Jochanaan! Well, I will suck it now. I will track it with my teeth!"

...and He-Rod approaching her from behind.

"Hoo-yah!"

After that show, Anne-Sophie went missing for weeks. The last anyone saw of her was at the wrap party, headed off to the "closet" with the grip and best boy ("Couple of weird cats," the stand-in cock told the Chief Inspector. "I think maybe they were retards... always wearing shoulder pads..."). Everyone supposed she just needed a break; the pressure was finally getting to her. She often stood in front of the mirror and ran her fingers along the snaky bulges, wishing she could push her nails beneath the roiling cords and cables, grab hold of them like weeds and yank them out of her for good. Or at least that's the way people interpreted her silences. In reality, she was thinking about Nästa, how she had failed him, how she had held on to her humanity like a series of whole notes instead of embracing his wonderful, wonderful vision. And suddenly she was confessing things to these mongoloid stagehands like they were angels, and they put reassuring hands on each of her shoulders.

"W-well, maybe w-w-w-we c-can help."

"We're b-b-big fans…"

"Sh-sure. F-f-follow us."

And somewhere deep beneath the City streets, Tragedy's hunchbacked twins shuffled through the effluent of over a million asses, leading their prize through the piss and stink to the big Greek himself. They'd been searching for Judith for months, ever since she ducked out on him at his exotic retreat and went back to Neil. The intense blueness of Tragedy's paradise sky had hurt her eyes. There was hardly any place she could go without getting sand between her toes. Plus, the spicy food was giving her the runs. And the sun's kiss had left her with a nasty burn. The bridge of her nose was also peeling, and the servants begged her to wear a *yashmak* to cover her face, if not for her virtue than for the prevention of skin cancer.

The scarves were Judith's saviour. With an endless supply of the things at her disposal, she conveniently "lost" one a day for nearly five months ("You must think me such an idiot," she would say to the women who supplied them to her, who she knew must be growing suspicious), fashioning a crude rope out of them, which she hid under her stack of mattresses. She was deathly afraid that her father would discover her, and paid close attention to his every move. Tragedy, regardless, was taking less and less notice of her, his attention more focused on one of the serving girls. On the two hundred and second day of her kidnapping, Judith took a peek into her father's room to make sure he was busy (Tragedy was under the maid's dress, nibbling at her thighs; "Such an interesting name," she was saying. "Were your parents— ow!—interested in drama...?"), fished out the *yashmak* rope, and silently withdrew through the window.

But before she disappeared, Tragedy had given her a gift—a pair of earrings—as a way of making historical amends ("I know I haven't always been the best dad... but... well... here you go..."). And eventually, after months of tracking her to North America, the homing beacon in one of those earrings led them straight to Anne-Sophie, the tiny earring in her chest sending out pulses of electricity that she could neither feel nor prohibit. Any gesture the twins made in the vicinity of the soprano buried the sensor's needle. And eventually they made the call that brought Tragedy back across the pond.

"That isn't her, you morons!"

"B-b-b-but the signal?!"

"Can't you even recognize your own freakin' sister? Drop the frog in a box and let's get back to work."

But after only a few hours of tracheal probing surgery (most instruments they pushed down there never came back the same), the big Greek's scientists managed to extract the gold-plated girandole from deep inside Anne-Sophie's windpipe. And gradually the story of how the earring got there came out. The beacon had led them to one of Judith's lovers after all. Tragedy smiled. Anne-Sophie, who was already shattering glass at two hundred and thirty feet, was strapped to the steel panel as Tragedy's doctors tinkered with her throat, drawing the lines for her new aryepiglottics and arytenoids, his engineers designing a new apparatus to replace her sarcomere, her epiglottis. As Tragedy put it, they were only giving her what she wanted, to become the biggest freak of them all, but the doctors shook their heads, cited prior failed experiments in the field of mechanical sternocleidomastoid research (mostly early cancer treatments, albeit on a much smaller scale), all failures, due to the supreme imbalance that was created between man and machine. Some of the metals (titanium, uranium, and mercury) caused severe memory loss and depression. Others (plutonium, kryptonite) precipitated the deterioration of other muscles, a result of the trapezius and pectorals being in direct contact with the unnatural *gorge méchanique*, much too electrically conducive, resulting in severe hyperflexion and then rapid atrophy. The body's immune system ultimately came up with guerrilla-type antibodies to fight the foreign elements inside it, corroding the new additions and poisoning the subject with rust.

And her throat was already so huge, larger than Tragedy's biceps; perhaps wider than her own waist. Reinforcing it, even if successful in the strictest experimental sense, might also be dangerous, fatal to her, or potentially volatile even, which put them all in peril. The hydraulics of the sarcomere in question were based on outdated nuclear and electrical principles. Stuff not even Clerval, one of the early pioneers in bionics with Ingolstadt AB, was willing to continue studying. If something went wrong, for example, if the jaw hinge were to be overworked, or if something jammed, like her new positronic vocal chords...

"Christ! What are you? A bunch of babies?"

Which was a difficult argument to oppose.

They went back to the drawing board. A new face, entirely rebuilt nose and jaw, telescopic vision, high-speed hamstrings and internally reinforced calliper splints, and a right arm with kung-fu grip, basically to keep up with everything they put inside her. Including a full laryngectomy, replacing the tissue with this new lunarium stuff, muscles with pistons and hydraulics, a stainless-steel epiglottal lid (to prevent corrosion), positronic laser eye-beam vocal chords. And a cordotomy for more unrestrained manoeuvrability, should she ever need to turn her noggin all the way round to her neddy, or even further, rotating monstrously, inexorably. It was considered almost a miracle when she opened that dull, yellow eye at all.

"She's alive! Sh-sh-she's alive!"

"Hoo-yah!"

Yet, because of Tragedy, Anne-Sophie lost what little humanity she once possessed. She'd been so transformed, was barely recognizable as the girl she once was. And when she finally showed up back at Nästa's apartment, he saw only the machinery, not the person underneath. He thought, *this must be the thing that took away my one true love Anne-Sophie, come back to claim me.* Dislocating every possible joint in his body, he slipped between the bars on his bedroom window and took off down the alley.

Her own wail took out most of the windows on the street. She was absorbing so much energy from the air around her that the street lamps dimmed. And she ended up crying rusty tears in an alley behind the church tower, her massive head cloaked in burlap with a single eyehole. She'd been fending for herself okay, consuming stones from the church's foundation for the minerals, chasing off nosy dogs and children, but everything above her shoulders now weighed so much that she couldn't sleep lying down. Tragedy's men had built special brackets into the wall of the lab where she could be braced and hung. But on her own she was forced to catch her winks propped up in a sitting position, with her head resting on her knees. Otherwise she thought she might never get up again.

It was getting so late. She felt so tired. This winter they were stuck in, it rubbed at her arms and ass, chilled her from shoulders to shins.

Her head nodded forward.

There was a charming snap.

The Tower

XX. Several misunderstandings

IT ALL CAME back to Judith, whom they all sought, then rebuffed, then sought again. But no one really understood her, which was why they discussed her so often at the Grad Lounge over games of Hearts. And statements did nothing to describe her. So they riffled their mental card catalogues for the proper metaphor.

"She moves like broken light..."

"...a poorly defined rainbow..."

"She's glass without cames," Booting suggested, dealing another hand.

"She's certainly hard to keep together," Marsh acknowledged, recalling his earlier attempts to draw her, resorting to thoughts of specific limbs (and sometimes unrelated objects) so that he could draw the whole. Fingers drawing hands, ears and banana peel lips drawing head, ribs and horse-yoke collarbone drawing breast.

And Marsh's current girlfriend Isabella, who likened Judith to a Warhol soup can ("One of a million, and totally without class...") and herself to a ballerina by Dégas ("A butterfly caught in the glare of the footlights..."), with her cigarette flaming like a blowtorch, jealous as all fuck (unaware of the presence of Dallas on the playing field at this point): "She's hard to keep from mentioning, that's for sure." Puff, poff; pissed-off, stargazing look. "Are you bidding, or what?"

When Neil saw her at the library, he turned to Burke for support, and the old poet dug deep to find the right words for the occasion, sentiments that had served him well before. Moonlit nights, the unsought snuggle, bodies passing with effort through water. Neil's delivery was all off ("...your lips are like bee stings..."). But there must have been something about him that attracted her. His words came out like trampled ants, hopelessly spinning and pinching, trying to work, yet without suitable functionality. And still she agreed to meet with him.

Then, for weeks and months, Neil couldn't believe how much Judith misunderstood him. She mistook his comfort for disinterest, his attention for analytical spite. They were having such a good time one night, discussing true love ("It seems to make sense to me that a person could madly, deeply, love more than one other. Concurrently, even. And because of that, no reason why anyone would remain socially exclusive..."), and all of a sudden she asked him to take her home. And not for one of their romantic sessions, either. When he saw the tears and asked what was troubling her, she slammed the door. That was that. Or so it seemed.

Even so, Neil managed to awaken something inside of her. When Judith and Booting first met, she was embarrassed by her lack of artistic accomplishment. "What is it that *you* do?" he asked her, the worst question she could possibly imagine, surrounded, as she was, by their collective creativity. She could hardly tell him that she was merely a receptionist at the University, not when everything Booting was working on seemed so daring and abstract. From that day onward, she made it her mission to mimic their artistic lifestyle, but after weeks and months of art lessons from Marsh, not even Burke had the heart to tell her that her canvases looked neglected and baggy, that she painted in fat gashes, or that her sense of colours seemed limited to river silt, muddy brown and glossy, like shit on vinyl. She felt as though every previous instant in her life had been utterly and entirely lost.

Of course, when Judith painted in her browns and blacks, the diarrhea-like artistic effluent was entirely deliberate. After all, she learned from the master of colours himself, the famous Dutch Dye-king: Venn. It was merely that, when Marsh told her to copy Matisse, she saw the dancing figures as dangling, and those dark stains were the only colours she could see.

Besides, it was not the style of the painting that attracted her, nor the subject, but the naming and the claiming of the work, the reality of the creator and the creator's identity as paramount. Art, she saw, could not exist without the artist, nor scientific discovery without scientist. Diseases and singularities, Picassos and Van Goghs, all named for the person who had discovered them. And so she began working more carefully on the names themselves, the signatures, the artistic nuclei, sketching a perfect Duchamp, or Mutt, or Sélavy, the theory being that, if she could figure out what made them, she might be able to reinvent herself, become more like them. She copied page after page of any name she could get her hands on, trying on each of them like a sinister cowl, then moved on to full pages of correspondence—as well as public addresses, order forms, letters of recommendation, recipes and office memos, minimalist fiction (a nearly illegibly scrawled "BOY MEETS GIRL"), grocery lists, carefully designed currency, and grad school applications—reproducing anything she saw with the precision of a photocopier.

There were even love letters from Neil (she'd been hiding them under her pillow, crying tears into them, kissing them and pressing them between her legs while she slept at night), although she'd written most of those to herself.

And once she had mastered someone utterly, she began to compose new thoughts and paragraphs for them, as the writers might have expressed them had they the time and good sense to think of them on their own. She became re-electrified with the idea of generating new life.

It was a talent she had inherited from her father, although instead of becoming cygnets, she adopted signatures. It was just such a pleasure to copy, such a special pleasure to see things born again, to see things inked out and recreated with complete identicity. And to be able to add to that... well... this would be her major contribution to the world. With her ballpoint in her fists, with the great brass nozzling tip spitting its seminal squid juice upon the world, the blood pounded in her head; and her hands were the hands of some amazing conductor playing all the symphonies of tracing and transcribing at once, to rebuild the tattered, ruinous canon of literature. More than anyone else, however, it was Neil who became her addiction. She needed more and more. And that appropriation of Neil's handwriting and voice were what led to the work she would become most known for. The novelist was working in fits, labouring for days and days before narcoleptically collapsing on the laboratory floor. And while he slept, she set upon his hastily scrawled notes, then flew away before the winds of morning could dampen the flame of her pursuits.

A lot of what he wrote, she didn't understand. His diaries (what else could they be called now, as much as he associated himself with the tower) were bloody with dark thoughts, dry corpses, and tremulous string music. And somehow she knew it was wrong, but she still tried to justify it: like Burke, she saw the fall of language in this winter (in Neil's rejection of traditional grammatical values to produce a list of literary merit), and creating for Neil was her attempt to "take up the slack of the literary tow rope." When it came right down to it, though, it was simply a way to get closer to Neil, that by re-writing every one of his words she might be able to see inside him, might come up with a reason for his negligence.

Of course, she had no idea what was going on in the catacombs beneath the tower, no clue that the book was only the tip of Neil's fractal iceberg. She could never have imagined Neil dabbling in the dirt like he was. Normally, when she climbed in through the window, he was passed out at his great desk, his lab coat billowing around his emaciated frame, hiding the blood and filth of his broken fingernails. So she imagined he was making all that corpse stuff up. But then, one night as she was tip-toeing past him, his eyes opened wide so suddenly. He grabbed her by the wrists. And he dragged her forcefully to the cellar.

"I've been expecting you."

That night, Neil showed her the bodies he had found, mother and child, the results of his forced solitude, the ways he had improved them, an army of skeletal soldiers just waiting for the breath of life. She was disgusted, repulsed; and not only with Neil, but also with herself. All her labouring, toiling with his writing. Purple passages like bruises on his highly abused texts. And this was what she was helping to spread? She had played a part in creating this monster? Sure, she had always been attracted to his dangerous side. But she wanted a boyfriend who was on the edge, not over it. This guy was a one hundred percent, certifiable wacko. He paraded before her like a frilly dandy (some kind of new fashion statement, she gathered, decked out in satin and silk), deftly tossed an errant skull into the air with the hook of his foot, and spoke to her by clacking the calcified mandible like chattering toy teeth, his own lips in an epileptic tremor. She dared not again raise her eyes to his face (nor the face of the poor, deceased soul in his hand), there was something so scaring and unearthly in his ugliness.

"These are the tombs, Jude! Am I, who proudly gaze on the construction and the skulls around, not to sum this mass of totality, to add up these mounds of mouldering flesh? This is human life! This is understanding!"

She could see how far he'd fallen, could make out each dent in his sanity.

XXI. A part of Booting, lost and revealed

JUDITH'S FAITH IN Neil was like a premonition. Neil's ship was coming in. And for Burke, it seemed as though Judith's belief made it so. She willed the novel's completion (from far away, of course, on a trip with her father, but the power of love is strong), dreamed up the contract, the revenue, thought of people coming to the book-signings. Also, he was lucky enough to be born in a time that suited his tastes, that praised the virtues of brevity and fact. *The Tower* emerged in a time when people were looking for the quick fix, more interested in the elements of the story than the story itself. So Neil's list, which began with an inventory of the characters and ended with an extensive list of every object unrelated to the tower's actual physical structure (*wires, worms, weirs, and words, a shard of broken glass, a small transistor, mouldy bread, old Life magazines, National Geographics, a bell, a bike, a book*), was accepted, nay, absorbed by both the public and the critics. A classic by a contemporary master, already included in several university course syllabi, the subject of more than a few doctoral theses, his name on the tip of every award-nominating tongue, the respect of his colleagues...

"A novel in stasis," it was being called. Daring and deliciously different.

"After only a few pages," one critic wrote, "you will find yourself engrossed by the irresistible force of this immovable abject. Neil Bauer's *The Tower* makes Beckett's *Murphy* look like an action hero."

Still others lauded the book as the most important novel—if it could still be called that—to be published in their lifetime: "If ever the story of any private man's imagination were worth making public, this is it!"

...to which almost all of his friends agreed. But, of course, most of them needed Neil's success to justify their own lives. They needed some proof that they weren't all striving for nothing, that they weren't all wasting their lives in what Booting would have called "the pursuit of intellectual atrophy." For Isabella, Marsh's Art History friend, it was enough to be part of the scene, to be there when it happened, so that one day she might be able to make use of her own degree, penning the biography of Neil's life during his sunny university days, when his prose was more carefree and flowing, when he wasn't so concerned with the curses of old writers: sentimentality, wars, character, plot.

"Carefree and flowing?" Marsh challenged her later in the car. "You don't know shit about writing."

"And you do? Neil speaks for an entire generation with his prose."

"It's just a list! He wrote a fucking list!"

"A list with feeling. It's tragic."

"Tragic like a dictionary!"

When they discovered Booting's cancer, Burke was the one who took him to the hospital. He'd been diagnosed with osteogenic sarcoma in his lower right leg, a cancerous tumour that made the bone go soft, and the feeling was like ants eating at his joints, a termitic of gnawing disabling the structural integrity of his leg. Within weeks, it became difficult to walk, the pressure of each step buckling the knee. The ground and gravity became his enemies. He walked like a singed insect. The doctor said it was important to get rid of it as soon as possible, to sacrifice the leg just above the knee, for the benefit of the rest of his body.

Booting sought other opinions. The cancer was not in doubt, but maybe another solution? His first idea was that he could just clone himself and replace the duplicate's limb for his own. Certainly there was some cloning precedent out there. They'd been doing it to sheep and mice for years. Many national armies were comprised solely of clones these days, weren't they? Booting had studied the preliminary equations laid out by the celebrated biologists Finney and Siegel, and even though he didn't have access to a nucleus extractor, or a DNA storage kit, it was pretty clear from what they'd written that all the fancy stuff they used was just to beef up the government-funded budget. Special effects to make it more appealing to the press. A religious cult in Québec was claiming to have done it through force of will. Some young kid at UCLA was bragging he could do it with a jackknife and camping stove. And Booting's own experiments fell somewhere in between, succeeding with some toenail clippings and a jar of fetal bovine serum he picked up on eBay from a frustrated group at NASA. By the time of the scheduled operation, one of the toenails had grown in size by about 16 percent. But there was barely a recognizable body part, even under a microscope. He even tried putting it in the microwave for about five minutes wrapped in tinfoil, but after the first few sparks he decided it might be simpler to just show up for the surgery.

By the time of Neil's celebration, Booting had grown even more sullen and depressed. Yet less disgusting. The only thing that seemed to cheer him up was that new opera he also went to with Burke. While Marsh held sway over most of Neil's guests wielding only his indifference, Booting ranted somewhere near the puff pastries about the loss of his leg to cancer: for fuck's sake, all of that business about still feeling anything was a bunch of poetic crap; the truth was that it was gone, and all you could feel was that it was gone. Plain and simple. Burke imagined that he knew how Booting felt, but it was Burke's heart that had been cut from him, amputated by Judith's declaration of feelings for Neil. He felt as though he might never be able to feel love again. Burke continued to drink himself to dissipation while the world of nostalgia, theory and cynicism spiraled around him.

"You don't get it because your basic concepts have been skewed by your education. You can't grasp the concept of author's intention because you see it as one thing, one meaning, not as the author's intent to fill a text with potential Meaning, many possible meanings all at once, with no all-encompassing, planned, kinetic Meaning at all..."

"...most kids these days can't even find their own ass-hole on a map..."

"I got one leg, fuck! Count 'em! One!"

It was Neil who brought the glazier momentarily out of his funk. The church had decided they wanted to update their windows with the new construction, and when the contractors approached the novelist to ask if he knew anyone who did that sort of thing, Booting was his immediate referral. If he could trust him to look after his manuscript, this was a no-brainer. And although Booting wasn't above playing the sympathy card (when he first met Marsh's new girlfriend Dallas, he tried to guilt her into rubbing his stump—"Sometimes I think I can even feel something, but I'm never sure, when I do it myself, if it's in my leg or my hand..."), he wasn't willing to ride Neil's coattails, either. When Judith left him, inspired by their nightly sessions, Booting spent longer and longer nights in the lab mixing sands, developing a glass that wouldn't require cames for its gravitational stability, that would also be permanent after the original vitrification, indestructible by force or heat. And he was sure this was the thing that would transform him into a household name, like Karl von Egeri or William Morris. Or even Louis Tiffany, who revolutionized the malleability of cames.

Despite earlier failures, Booting recognized the key had to be found in the proper combination of ingredients. So, having already exhausted the traditional periodic table, he tried other chemicals, like the rash of elements newly isolated in Europe: Magnium (Ma), Lunarium (Lu, used mostly in the manufacture of a new, durable, machinery alloy using the same name), Paracelsium (Pr) and Brightium (Tx). Each of them possessed conducive qualities that were previously unheard of, and while they had generally been wasted in the manufacture of useless automatons, video games, and robot dogs, if the glass could be made to have heat pass through it without breaking down its complex structure, it would certainly also take on the properties Booting was looking for. And so he persisted, his crackled visage lit up by the University Physical Plant's furnace ("Heat! I need more heat!"), drawing red-faulty heaves from the fiery hand of Knowledge.

Not that these elements were easy to come by. He'd wasted months on the more readily available Plutonium and Uranium. And frustrated, at the approach of loneliness and half two, he would sneak out of his lab a completely different man, to cultivate the society of the underdogs and prostitutes: the strip bars with their mat-tressed back rooms, the peep shows (pornographic films for a quarter, with titles like *New Arabian Nights*, *The Black Arrow*, *The Wrong Box*, *Oh La-la...*), an X-rated opera, and the local freak show. The poster out front—all over the City—displayed a beautiful, young woman, a pistol aimed directly in her face (*Come Inside for the REAL Deep Throat!*). And it was here that he caught wind of his eventual source, this place, a gathering of all the City's seediest elements, this pit, a culture where everything was available for a price. A couple of teenagers with backpacks beckoned him to follow, and Booting followed on his new prosthetic shin in a hunched, lurching gait.

"Get it? Walk this way?"

"..."

"Whatever... Do you take Visa?"

"Sh-sh-shure we do."

"Or M-M-Mastercard!"

The final mixture ("Add a dash of Brightium...") was at first of a reddish hue, and then began, in proportion as the crystals melted, to brighten in colour, to effervesce audibly, and to throw off small fumes of vapour; sudden-ly, and at the same moment, the ebullition ceased, and the compound changed to a dark purple, which faded again more slowly to a watery green. The resulting mass spilled out like grayish horsehair at his feet, the fibres straightening and aligning, exuding as slowly as moving lava. The gray substance met the air, lightened and whitened, then compressed into a dense, lumpy form. He was alive! But after that—the whole process took only a few moments—there was no way to shape the junk. Even his diamond cutter shattered at minimal contact. And the addition of any colouring agent only succeeded in breaking down the cohesive properties of the translucent concoction, making it useless to him in every way. He managed to make a tidy sum by selling the formula online to a graduate physics student from Texas or Tennessee or someplace, but then he just gave the whole thing up.

"What good is a clear lump of shit to me?" he spat. "I might as well go into the paperweight business."

The freaks, on the other hand, became the characters of Booting's artistic mythology, the freaks and downtrod-dens of his translucent *oeuvre*, and it was only natural that he bring them into his designs for the new church windows. Mary like a mountain, chawing on loaves and fishes. John the seal-boy Baptist. A self-portrait as some Irish saint with a wooden leg and a face like a ham. And most disturbing for the church committee, Christ with nails piercing every square inch of his body, surrounded by cross-eating freaks, two contortionist thieves, a giant ape, a little hunchbacked gothic gnome in the corner. He had managed to infuse them with such emotion: fear, abandon, longing. And perhaps most impressive was his plan to string several other windows between the sanctu-ary's nave and the neck, suspended horizontally directly above the pews, so as the sunlight grazed its way across the weddinged walls, the shades on the floor met and mixed, creating a shifting kaleidoscope of colours traditionally unachievable, occasionally meeting in a white both pure and saintly.

When he finished, the committee was mostly silent.

"The gnome is interesting," Neil offered, " I think." But they were obviously coming from diametrically opposed philosophies. The committee wanted something more contemporary, something to reflect the church's new acclimated adaptability, their hip-ness, but Booting refused, citing an artist's code of some sort.

"I mean no disrespect to your work, Mr. Booting, but we were thinking more about abstracts, pleasant shapes that announce the Word of God."

And Booting showed them the shape of his asshole.

XXII. Inspiration, investigation, motivation

WHAT REALLY FASCINATED Booting about the entire project were the tower's original windows, with their impressive use of thick camature and delicate grisaille, and their deep-seated sexuality. The construction crews had already stored the old windows in the kitchen for safekeeping while they did their thing, and the lack of direct sunlight had a curious effect on them, seemingly giving them even more depth. He spent days and hours in front of one in particular, merely sitting in front of it, watching it grow old, learning it intimately. He knew every square inch, from Mary Magdalene's exposed ankles and knees (certainly a risqué move a hundred and fifty years ago) to the queerly drawn tablets in her hands, like she had somehow replaced Moses in the mind of the artist, but with stones that looked startlingly like paper. Essentially, the techniques he used in making stained glass were the same as they had used since the twelfth century. But it was these strange choices, not the style or execution, that he found most confusing. All females, from Eve to Ruth to all the Marys. And even then, not the normal depictions of the church's blessed matriarchs, meek and mild, full of grace; something about them stood out; they were powerful, hair like cloaks, eyes like black rocks, and muscular...

Neil couldn't see it.

"Jesus Christ, Neil! Look at those roasts on the ends of her arms!"

It was true. Mary, the Mother of God, had hands the size of footballs. And behind her, on a hill in the background, some kind of metal machine.

"A cow, perhaps."

"A what?!"

The Towering Infernal, they were now calling Neil in the headlines. He so rarely left the tower that photos of him had become a commodity, and the reporters with their blue-balled cameras kept vigil in the graveyard for weeks, sometimes scaling the walls with suction cups Velcroed to wrist and knee (two chumps from *The Weekly World News* had already been escorted to hospital with multiple fractures), hiding behind gravestones, or in his garbage cans ("He's gotta get rid of his trash somehow..."), all for the front page scoop. Thank God for easily bought sources or they'd have no punnish nickname for him at all! Leaks from inside Neil Bauer's sanctuary (the Russian cleaning lady/audio bugging expert; those supposed chess-club kids with their miniature Black Queen spy cameras; even the gravedigger accused him of pilfering his shovels and mild explosives) said he had worked his way down to the sub-basement, had found something remarkable there in the dirt floors and skittle bugs, and everyone latched on to this downward motion like a falling star. The focus was set. The heights—the glamour—had made Neil famous. Could he sustain that popularity in an unfinished basement?

The headlines shifted—mostly uninformed speculations about the possibility the famed author was actually digging up bodies down there—from the simple, yet punchy, *Grave Plots* to the slightly more elaborate—and equally horrible—*A Matter of Corpse!* Yet the article credited with nailing the lid on the initial story was *The Hole Story: Getting the Real Dirt on Neil Bauer*, a two-page background spread by *The Tribune-Post*'s Head Reporter. In it, he endeavoured to pry into Neil's past (he'd recently been expelled from his doctoral program for linguistic heresy), his vices (he once ate an entire box of Contac-C, biked home, and ended up in a ditch), and included a short interview with Judith:

T-P: Where are you? Where is he?

J: I don't know...

...which didn't tell him so much, but after the interview ("I'll probably call you next week to do some fact checking..."), he followed her at a safe distance through the graveyard, and discovered the dark basement window she used to get at Neil's secrets. And that night he felt his way blindly through the murk, armed only with a tape recorder and camera, his mic cord coiled at his hip, a partial map of the tower's ground floor in the breast pocket of his leather jacket. Nothing compared to the darkness Booting would one day find himself in (every light in the galaxy extinguished by ignorance, unsure of which way was back), but still soupy enough to make the Reporter feel uneasy. One of his two guides (locals who had once helped out with Communion, who had skipped Sunday school to investigate the structure's secret corners) had abandoned him out of fear at the cemetery gates, taking all the lamps and flashlights. So he was forced to rely on what natural light existed. What little sunlight broke through the cracks in the walls was pale and milky in colour, and the room was darkly verdant (the moulds and mosses made his allergies act up), secretive, menacing: a seemingly infinite hexagonal gallery, five long shelves per side, shelf after shelf, with glass jar after glass jar, full and warm and lidded.

"Enough, guy," his remaining guide breathed. "Let us go back." But he was too close, was unprepared to let Belloq scoop the story for the *Zeitung*, and so pushed one of the lids back, instantly struck by what he imagined to be the scent of centuries, the trapped odours of years of silence and darkness. At one of the hexagon's points he found a torch and struck a match to it, and— "Oh, my Lord..."—gasping for air, tried to scream. Along with his experiments in lexical and corporeal reconstruction, Neil had become obsessed with several other things: among them, artistic effluence. He'd started collecting his shit in jars, spent days eating foods of the same colour—specifically foods with artificial dyes like Smarties, freezies, and soda pop—in order to generate the gradual prismic effect the Head Reporter upset all over his shirt (a mixture of cinnamon hearts and chili powder, Kool-Aid crystals and raspberries). He nearly threw up. He ran in place. And on his frantic dash back to the window, he tripped over the dead bodies Neil had re-assembled into a more perfect being (twelve feet high, with four legs for greater stability, skin made of recycled paper, hair slick and wet from skinned rats), and landed smack in front of the greatest journalistic prize he could have imagined.

The original hand-written manuscript.

Suddenly, cover stories around the globe were insinuating that Neil never wrote the book at all, that he stole his ideas from underground fiction, ancient texts he literally caused to rise again from the earth. The proof? *The Tribune-Post* claimed not to have found Neil's first stab at *The Tower* after all, but what was actually the source of Neil's manuscript. Before he abandoned his client, Giesler claimed it was one of Neil's own duplicates ("For safe keeping, you know..."). They had found it in the tower, hadn't they? But the paper on which it was purportedly written was judged to be some two hundred years old, the ink (an anachrony, to be sure) likewise. An investigation was started.

Then it suddenly started popping up everywhere,

each judged to be older than the last, unearthed by Fox television in an old Egyptian tomb ("Folks, you're not gonna believe this one!"), worn by a tribe of aborigines in Australia as loincloths, and discovered by a researcher at Oxford among Shakespeare's notes for *Hamlet*. It seemed as though a new one were popping up every few minutes, dug up by some great moor dog (so the locals whispered), or by mining robots on Mars (so the engineers swore, pointing franticly at the hazy images sent back via satellite). Charges were laid. And pretty soon the lawyers for the prosecution were able to show how the book was actually the notes for an early dictionary, that it was already being studied by university students in Eastern Canada. Identical in every way, they began piling up on the evidence table until the jury was forced to stand on tiptoe just to follow the rest of the proceedings. The lawyers pointed at the books on the table (some of the later editions even had covers drawn by Marsh, which no one could explain), and asked Neil if they were his.

"The books are all mine," was the answer, cold and remote. "And I have written more."

"Do you claim them all, or do you care to reject a part?"

"The books are mine..."

It was hopeless. No testimony was ever tested, no claims clarified, no statements starified in the eye. In his mind, Neil began to separate himself from the proceedings, as if they were talking about someone else. Even before he was arrested, the rest of them had begun to think of him as a bit of a loose nut. His hair struck out at strange angles. Something he was eating was constantly changing the colour of his tongue. Plus, he was absentminded (appointments completely slipped his mind, thus he spent more time than he had intended in the tower), clumsy (before he knew it, he had broken four of the bike's spokes). He would stumble into the Grad Lounge on a weekday afternoon, crashing over tables and chairs, upsetting the delicate imbalance of their 5.5 percent system, calling them all to action:

"If fiction exists only as ideas and meanings, what is there to separate it from other media like film or music?" Where was the quantitative measure of virtuosity? Were writers just hack philosophers expressing their own views on the universe? He would create fiction, not as a representation of reality, nor as a social theory, but as an equation. He wrote on walls as the ideas came to him, and the apartment he shared with Judith was riddled with phrases and strange linguistic tallies, combinations of words no one else had yet considered, destroying the common grammatical syntax across the dining-room table, along the baseboards, in closets and cupboards. That was how he first developed the idea that he might create physical being through precise inscription, a tower constructed purely from his gestating lexicon. "Words!" he shouted at them. "I can make anything I want now! Out of words!"

"Oh, come on!" Marsh protested. "If he could do that, he could have destroyed the Earth! Could have created new galaxies!"

Neil had delved under the secret streets of Reality and emerged mutated. He was ill. And now his world was tumbling around him. His literary discoveries had made him one of the most powerful men in the world, but when word came out that the book was not his, the public was quick to denounce him as a charlatan, a faker who had perpetuated the greatest hoax of all time. Was this what he called Art? A halt was placed on the next reprint (which sent collectors clambering for the last edition, and high-school students to the Internet to see what the fuss was all about). His investments were seized pending the trial, should he be required to pay every cent back to the readers who had placed their trust in him.

The only people who seemed to be in support of Neil—other than Marsh's ex-girlfriend Isabella, who only saw the potential for this whole scandal to play into her sales once her biography was finished—were the academics, always looking for some new lens through which they could re-examine the expanding mass of literature. One grad student from California even began publishing her own pilfered stories in some of the country's more established literary quarterlies, dropping Bukowski on *The New Yorker*, *The Book of Matthew* on *Harper's*, slipping Beckett's "The Smeraldina's Billet Doux" by *Playboy* as a purely autobiographical work. In interviews with the hip culture magazines like *Wallpaper**, *Superficial^*, or the Swiss *Teknoföhn*, she even went so far as to tag plagiarism as the only valid form of expression left to a credible writer. Visual artists had been doing it for years. And it remained the only way for writers to escape their egos, sense of narrative, their urges towards the Romantic, and the smallness of their own minds. *Teknoföhn*, not one to report on a new trend without wholly embracing it, ran it as a cover headline (*I Didn't Do It... but I might as well have...*), but then reprinted an unrelated article by Mark Twain on the inside without a word of explanation or acknowledgment. And in an article published on the eve of the trial, their resident culture critic predicted Neil would actually beat the rap, which would have enormous repercussions on copyright laws around the world, not to mention on the classroom. It was a tough pill to swallow, perhaps, but that was what the kids were doing these days, and if the orthodox publishers couldn't wake up to that, they were headed the way of the dinosaurs. As an exercise for her students ("A lesson in life," she said), the Californian had them not write papers but hunt for them, seeing who could plagiarize the best essay on Eliot's "The Waste Land."

Cutting and pasting from several texts was not only permitted but encouraged.

She defended her practice before her university's senate: "Any text is the absorption and transformation of another. Nothing I can say, no word, not even a gesture of the head is without a predecessor. Books have been sleeping with each other for years. Neil Bauer has just helped them come out of the closet."

It became more and more impossible to believe in his innocence, what with the biased press, the circumstantial evidence, his habit of flip-flopping on the issues. Neil was unreasonable. More than slightly unbalanced. He enjoyed playing the martyr so much that he confessed to everything with which he was confronted. Not that Neil's assigned lawyer was doing anything to help the writer's cause. For the most part, he kept silent, studying a particularly interesting knot in the table before him, occasionally leering at the stenographer, sniffling and snorting. He urged Neil to keep silent as well, and only really made his presence known when the back doors suddenly burst open and they wheeled Tragedy into court in full body cast and catheter. The only people who really mattered to Neil's future were the jury, a motley collection of recluses and halfwits, narrowed down from several hundred by natural selection (due to Neil's growing celebrity, jurors were weeded out using literacy tests, only the lowest scores asked to return). And Tragedy had them from the beginning, winning over most of their votes before he even reached his seat. The poor man, all of his injuries caused directly, he claimed, by Neil Bauer's blatant disregard for his readers. Several of the male jurors winced visibly at the 13" catheter protruding from between his legs (really just his own wrapped penis, the prosecution figuring it was the only way to hide it *and* make it work for them), while the women—they had pushed for a female majority during the selection process—shifted uncomfortably in their seats, suddenly flushed. And Neil's lawyer raised his arms so high that he nearly fell over backwards, thrown off balance as he was by the huge backpack he insisted on carrying beneath his robes:

"R-right on!"

This, at last, was Tragedy's revenge. Just as he got back at Anne-Sophie, and Booting, and was even the one to tip the Menzies clan off to the whereabouts of his daughter and Venn. Now he had Neil. To have laboured so hard, to sincerely quest for the betterment of humanity, and then have everything yanked out from underneath him... It was more than any sane person could take. People were angry at having been duped. And while it was strange that no prior record of the book existed in any anthologies or bibliographies (Burke devoured everything from the *Oxford Guide* to Holbrook Jackson, searching for some kind of clue), the evidence against him seemed unquestionable, irrefutable. Once the books were brought before the Court, it took very little time to bring down a verdict. And as a precaution—the psychiatric ward had found Neil to be particularly violent in the past—they brought in the army. They burst through the door as the verdict was read ("We find the defendant, Neil Bauer..."), dressed in white to blend in with the courtroom walls, knocking over lamps and spreading along the walls like blown cotton.

Camouflaged in wood-panelling khakis, they seeped out of the pine jury stand. They threw down disguises of reporters, stenographers, blind men, elderly women. They had guts. They had guns.

But Neil was already defeated. At times, he seemed completely oblivious to what was going on around him. His emotions were so carefully considered, delayed. His reactions seemed dull, inattentive. He felt like a stranger, or an outsider, analyzing his thoughts and actions as though they were someone else's. Only Judith's testimony appeared to get a rise out of him, and even then it was as if he were acting more out of expectancy than will. He had asked her to admit what she'd done, that the copies were actually—somehow—hers. But when she eventually took the stand, she was so clearly her father's daughter, presenting her own version and said that was the only one she had made. Neil grunted, swung his arms, beat his chest, and then settled back into his chair as if he'd played his part and exited stage left. But Neil was their voice, and everyone was looking to him to make sense of it all. It was up to him to justify what he had done, to give meaning to an act without sense. Well, then. Perhaps he was the monster they made him out to be, or the mad scientist, or the criminal. And they could judge him. They could punish him. But in the end, he'd just been trying to make himself a better person. To make them all better people. To save them. Did that not count for something? By breaking down the tower into all of its composite parts, Neil was only trying to reveal a little bit of the Truth in their lives. He was just trying to bring them complete understanding. And for a moment in that courtroom, as he spoke his piece, struggling against the restraints ("Maybe you should look at the monster inside each of you!"), his soul was elevated from its debasing and miserable fears, to contemplate the divine ideas of liberty and self-sacrifice, of which these pages were remembrances. For an instant, he dared to shake off his chains, to rise up and look around himself with a free and lofty spirit. But the guilt had eaten into his flesh, and he sank again, trembling, hopeless, into his miserable self.

He was quickly coming to the realization that no one else wanted to understand. They were happy with their faith and murmurs, their longing and their enigmatic allegory. By capturing the tower so succinctly, Neil had separated it from the Magic that had made it so special to them in the first place.

He had done this all for them. Didn't they see...?

"I am alone."

Unnatural.

How else could one explain it?

Marsh and Dallas

XXIII. Overtaken by catastrophe

MARSH STARTED TAKING pictures of Judith when she asked him to teach her the finer nuances of chess, a game she found most abhorrent for its lack of accomplishment (if there was no actual ground gained, just an imaginary battlefield, what was the point?), not least because her grasp on the rules was immature at best. In the middle were various other things (that Swedish musical, for one). And despite the fact that Marsh made it a rule not to teach things to anyone (at least not directly), he agreed to it. The catch? In exchange for learning chess, she would have to model for him. A roll of film for each lesson, each gambit or defense strategy learned.

A deal.

"If you could just sit down over there, then, on the edge of the bathtub, we can start right away." And not too much anticipation now... "Would you mind, um, removing your blouse?"

Which she didn't. Mind, that is. It was all in the name of art, after all.

"Yes, right."

Before he knew it, she was in the bathtub instead of sitting on its edge, and the camera was back in its case, and his hair was wet, water down his back, in his mouth, in his boots, and one of her breasts was in his hand (like he'd been dreaming about ever since she'd cut loose on him at that party), and a hand on his prick, his nuts, fingers licking across his scalp, his chest, his nuts, a tongue in his mouth that was not his own, and his own tongue travelling the cleft of her ass, the faucet mining uncomfortably into his back, but silvered lips on his nipple all the same, on his neck, his ear, his nuts!

He would need regular massages for the rest of his life.

Then Judith moved in. Marsh's latest model, an Art History major named Isabella, was forced to spend her afternoons either watching them play chess or talking to that moron Burke. The ever-hovering Burke. Documenting the world in his little notebook, who only talked about things like the coast or voices or—what the fuck!?—poetry. Nothing real, only peripheral, if he could be convinced to speak at all, which was rare, his nose practically up the ass of Marsh's newest little bitch. Sometimes it was as if he wasn't even paying attention, just staring off into space and writing whatever it was that came into his head. "That girl has all the grace of a painting by Kandinsky," Isabella said when Judith went to the store, stripping in front of Marsh for her bath, his camera limp, dormant on top of the refrigerator. "Her smile is a broken fence by Wyeth. Her hair is tangled yarn. I've seen more shapely tits on a Picasso. And do you see this photo you took of her holding the croquet mallet?"—Judith, nude except for a pair of striped, mid-thigh leggings and a hair ribbon, Marsh's cat nuzzling her foot—"Her arms would have more grace with her elbows swiveled into her ribs, slightly hyper-extended. And her waist wouldn't look so thick if she would just turn her hips three-quarter. She obviously knows nothing about art."

But the photos were simple, and developed into his first real exhibition. He never intended to do anything with them, just take them out to look at every once in a while. But the show was widely praised. The ruthlessness and sensuality of games. The human body as arena. He was depicting reality, which had suddenly come back into fashion after all these years. Bravo!

Isabella was gone when he came back from the bakery the next morning. She took the television.

Unlike Isabella, however, who could play chess competitively with Marsh after only a few weeks, Judith was not a great student of the chess duel, failing consistently to follow even his four basic opening tenets. She answered his pawn to king-four appropriately with one of her own, and his knight to king's bishop-three with a pawn to queen-three, but when he slid his bishop to the fourth position, she countered with another pawn to king's rook-three. Even Burke's eyebrow went up. But Judith took no notice at all, continuing to move pieces that had Marsh increasingly disgusted. Kt-B3; B-Kt5? What the...?

"The knights, Judith! What about the goddamn knights?!"

Marsh tried to teach her various strategies: the Morphy and Steinitz Defenses, the Queen's Gambit (also Declined), Evans Gambit, and even Endon's Affence. But his lessons still refused to take hold. He allowed Judith the first move and then mirrored her. They exchanged knights. And her game progressed smoothly until she placed her queen's bishop at the king's knight-five. "A mistake!" Marsh hollered. "You ought to guard against the threatened knight to knight-five with your bishop to king-two. Now you are overtaken by catastrophe!"

Indeed, they both were.

XXIV. The physicist's dream

"SHE'S USING YOU," came the warning, but this from Isabella, who couldn't seem to get it through her head that he had hoofed her out of his studio last week, that her opinions were no longer requested... that he had hoofed her out of the studio last week!

"Holy fuck, Iz, do you think I don't know that she's using me? Am I some kind of fucking idiot?"

Because all she could offer was that Judith was using Marsh to get to Neil, when that was the exact same reason why Isabella herself stayed so close. And he'd been with her for years!

"I'm only stating the obvious, Marsh."

"And I'm only asking you to bring back my fucking TV. So help me, Iz, this whole thing is purely platonic. She's in need. She's my friend. Am I supposed to turn her out on the street?"

And that night Judith needed him inside her, needed him to paint her body with acrylics that cracked and peeled but left stains in her pores like bruises.

"Who's this Venn guy you keep talking about?"

Of course, all anyone else saw—they were lax with their window blinds, and Burke had become adept with mirrors and lenses—was that Judith and Marsh were banging each other. And they all carefully assumed the couple were in love, which was certainly not the image Marsh was trying to convey when he was trying to hook up with that scientist from Texas he'd seen with Neil's agent at the book launch. How had a grease-basted porker like him, his gut full of stuffing and his hair like streams of gasoline, managed to land her? The movement of his porcine machinery across the room was peaked and clatterous, propelled ploddingly by the crank and sigh of each pistoning leg. He trailed the residue of his flatulence behind him like exhaust. And she... Dallas! She was otherworldly, with the mixed unease and snobbish posture of the socially alienated, resulting in a cascading sort of pout. She smelled like extinct flora. And silent, so silent.

Dallas entered their universe like a shooting star, with her red hair trailing destructively behind her. By far, she had the most amazing tail he'd seen in his life. And the male population fell like unsuspecting dinosaurs. What are you? May I bite you? Eat you? She seemed genuinely impressed with Neil's conversation, but who wouldn't? He was the only successful one among them. Booting tried to guilt her into rubbing his stump ("Sometimes I think I can even feel something, but I'm never sure, when I do it myself, if it's in my leg or my hand..."). And because he was powerless to do anything else (he'd volunteered to help out by handing out name tags at the door), Marsh put his own name on her, and followed her like a bad case of hemorrhoids.

At first, she didn't even notice. Dallas was used to existing with someone else's name, especially a man's. Her parents, Clifton and Emily, line workers at the Dr. Pepper plant on Legacy Drive in the Dallas suburb of Plano, had named her, strangely enough, not after their hometown, but after Dallas Frazier, Grammy Award winner and Nashville Hall-of-Famer. It was Frazier's "Honky Tonk Downstairs" that George Strait recorded as the B-side to "I Just Can't Go On Dying" in '76. He'd also written songs for other country greats like George Thorogood and Emmylou Harris. Clifton met her mother at the company picnic in Dublin, behind the baseball stands, where they were both throwing up after over-agitation, guzzling company wares like water before and after running the bases. She was like something out of the movies, her role mostly silent, and her cut-off jeans so short you could practically see her navel. He had the good sense to wipe his mouth and take another good swig of the Pepper before kissing her. The time (Dallas was a product of Time, and it ran her entire life more than her biological parents ever would) just seemed right. When it became increasingly clear there was something growing inside of her, Cliff and Em both remembered hearing Frazier's pop favourite "Alley Oop" over the loud speakers. She wasn't a boy ("Well, what can you do?"), but by then they had already grown so attached to having a star in the family. So the name stuck.

She was, however, a brilliant child ("What Bright weren't?" beamed her parents in tandem). At the age of three, she used her crayons to demonstrate a Möbius strip, a one-sided piece of paper some felt held the secret to four-dimensional travel. By six, she had discovered how to manipulate the strips into a Klein bottle, a supposedly theoretical 4-d container based on the same principles as Möbius's discovery. She got the idea from Dr. Seuss's classic tale about *Marvin K. Mooney*: *On a paradox pedaler / You can travel through time / You can turn inside out with a bottle by Klein*. And to her it was nothing more than copying what she saw in the book. But for her father, to whom good ideas came so rarely, it was a clear opportunity to introduce a brilliant new gimmick to the world of refreshments: Klein's Drink. Each drink would be packaged in its very own paradox, a Klein bottle without the separation of inside and outside, the label covered in other puzzles of science. They would feature flavours like Newton's Carbonated Apple Juice, and Esher-ade. The advertising campaign would centre around historical figures coming to quench the thirst of modern-day kids, Mozart crashing through the wall of the symphony hall ("Oh, yeah!"), rescuing parched concert-goers from dehydration and from boredom, tearing a few licks on his Strat, winking at the camera for the delivery of the final tagline: "Ein-ah Klein-ah Pop is Fine-ah!" The only problem occurred when a machine could not be devised for Klein manufacture. It was, after all, a four-dimensional principle, far beyond the abilities of three-dimensional robots. Only Dallas herself seemed able to master it, and she knew nothing yet of mechanics, quantum or otherwise.

"For Pete's sake, Clifton, she *is* just a child..."

"What do they teach her in that darned kindergarten of hers?!"

Marsh and Dallas barely spoke the first night they saw each other. But he went home unable to forget the way she smelled; she went home unable to forget his name. And then she called him a week later ("Well, I still had that name tag, and I would have called sooner, but I thought there might be more than one Marsh in the book..."), with tickets to a lecture by her old friend Doctor Wonmug, at the University, on the universe's incapacity for infinite cosmic strings ("Sounds great, huh?"). And afterwards, they talked for hours beneath the street lights.

D: "You know, I think the centre of mass representation he's proposing is invalid..."

M: "That guy had the biggest fucking feet I've ever seen!"

Miss Dallas Bright, whose eyes were like light, and when they met in the night, it was magic. Marsh had always been a confirmed bachelor, a loner, and the solitary brilliant hero with a mind untuned to the current state of civilization. For years his life had been in stasis ("Jesus, Iz, when are you going to cook dinner for once?"), the comfortable mimesis of normal life ("Want to rent a movie tonight?"), but his relationship with Dallas progressed with a Doppler effect, becoming more and more intense as they grew closer, and she inspired him to produce some of his finest work. Her mind crackled audibly with the sheer volume of synaptic explosions, and her ideas were speculative yet remotely palpable, as if they were words on the tip of the universe's tongue, just waiting to be spat into being. She never modelled for him (something he would later regret), and when they were alone, it was Dallas who did most of the talking, painting visions of a future world, complete with eternal youth, satellite courage, online self-esteem, and automatic back scratchers. "We're really just a mishmash of electrical impulses and signals," she said. "A miniature subway system enclosed in flesh, and no one can really figure it out yet. There's no map on the wall, no guide, and about fifty million different lines, so it's understandable that even the most brilliant scientist could get lost. But when someone does map those synapses, which can only be a few years away judging by the breakthroughs made recently by Temple Bell and the scientists at U.S. Robots, artificial intelligence on the same level as the human brain will become as commonplace as email. A positronic brain. A beta-wave replicator. A bionic encephalon. It doesn't matter. It will be nothing for the scientists of the future to replicate human thought waves and patterns, and for these new brains to work at one hundred percent..."

For once, he would go for the smart one, not the drunk in the short skirt, or the one Booting had his eye on.

"This subway system of yours," he put his hand on her knee. "Do you know how to get *off* yet?"

Marsh couldn't get enough of her, her fantastic stories and theories. Like how she'd studied under Dr. Ymer Framtiden, the half-Icelandic/half-Swedish professor of Physics who had made such waves recently with his invention of the time machine. She'd been there when he settled on a revolutionary new metal alloy called Lunarium for the hull. Dallas even helped name the capsule: *Audhumla* (a slightly anglicized version by Dallas of the Swedish words for "stream" and "hopper"). And when the prototype STÅ (*system tidsåterfående*/time retrieval) version returned from its trips with such conclusive evidence (untainted soil, the spoor of giant crabs, a videotape of something resembling a huge, white butterfly disappearing over some low hillocks), she was the one who helped him analyze and document it. Ymer didn't want to be too hopeful until the full-scale, piloted machine was tested. But when it returned successfully, its windshield splattered with prehistoric insects as big as your head, Framtiden's jumpsuit covered in the dust of paradox, it became impossible to contain what he had discovered.

If it hadn't all happened in Sweden, things might have gotten out of control even sooner. The tests would have generated an international uproar before Framtiden got a chance to even take it out again. As it stood, instead of inducing an ethical tizzy (Sweden was neutral, after all), or even a question of the machine's veracity (this was the land of Vikings and dragons, a people well used to the fantastical), there was a huge debate in the Stockholm press about what the machine should be used for. Hard-nosed social democrats thought a premature rescue of assassinated Prime Minister Olof Palme might save the crumbling government. Many polls showed that, if Palme were to run in the next election, his party would take eighty-two percent of the vote, a number unheard of in the contemporary Swedish twenty-nine (eight major) party system. And both Channel 1 and 2 began showing, in simulcast, never before seen footage from the 1989 Petterson trial (Channel 3 continued to show pop music videos). A few letters to the editor, under the auspices of a Scandinavian supremacy faction called the Swedish Covenant Control Authority, suggested returning to the days of the Vikings, convincing Erik the Red of the economic benefits involved with the early colonization of North America, transforming the northern blondes into world leaders, their rightful spot in the political food chain. But most suggestions were for an honest-to-God Jurassic Theme Park, complete with the "dinosaurs" they made up for the film. And the University, quick to take advantage of Ymer's discovery, hired a camera crew to go back in time to its own groundbreaking ceremony, for use in a new CD-ROM to replace the old, outdated calendar. Filmed entirely in black and white documentary style, it was the Chancellor's plan to then colourize himself in a brilliant scarlet—just a wee *pojke* back then—to mark the historic impact of the event on himself.

Of course, Framtiden had designs of his own. Every physicist's dream. And while the rest of the country debated what to do next, he continued working in secret. At last, a way to witness the formation of the planets, the expansion of the universe in reverse, even to be there for the first hundredth of a second! With Dallas as his assistant, he spent months planning his trip, perfecting his formulas, composing extensive cross-referenced lists, packing and repacking for optimum spatial benefit, setting the timers for his home lights. The University scheduled a second test for him, inviting both the press and the royal family, and he agreed, nodding without listening when they suggested a destination, then setting the dials exactly how he wanted them. Armed with gallons and gallons of water and sunblock, he hoisted himself through the udder-like hatch of his brave *Audhumla*, blew a kiss to his sweet Dallas (tossing her his ring as a promise of marriage on his return), and waved one last time to the University's gathered élite.

He exalted: "Yesterday, I shake hands with God!"

...which was often misquoted.

The story was in the news for many months. A new rash of time travel novels hit the shelves. Most bookstores had to expand their science fiction sections to keep up with it. Both the Americans and the Russians (according to spies) boosted their science budgets. They moved funds from social safety nets and new energy source research to specially disguised government foundations, like The American Cancer Foundation and The Ponds Institute. The Space Race was replaced by the Time Climb. And the U.S. President revved up his people in his annual State of the Union:

"Who needs to worry about energy any more? If this goes through, we can keep using the same litre of gas we put in the car the day before, over and over and over again!"

Applause.

"I don't mind telling you," the President almost giggled as an aside. "It's all pretty cool."

Unfortunately, Framtiden and *Audhumla* were never seen again. The Icelandic press, cashing in on his half-breed status, and careful to market this tragedy to the benefit of their generally ignored nation, made him out to be a legend. Dallas, her dark eyes and brilliant red hair making her the object of every Scandinavian's lust, went into the stories as Framtiden's Penelope, vowing to wait till the end of time for her precious Ymer to return from its beginning. It was a way to explain the cold shoulder she gave Sweden's Crown Prince, who approached her after the ceremony with an invitation to his private disco, and to Lars Larsson, the drummer and frontman for the heavy metal band *King Kung*. Back in Sweden, Dallas never once denied what she read in the *Dagens Nyheter*, but there were still parts of the story she wouldn't even divulge to Marsh.

XXV. Quantum relationships – when he looked for her, she was gone

IT WAS ALMOST as though they were of the same mind, how excited they both got about his paintings, and how much he contributed to her quantum studies without really knowing heads or tails about it. The machines he designed for her in his paintings were things of imagination and innovation. He took what she worked with and expanded upon it with the power of metaphor.

Thank God he was an expert on just about everything!

Marsh, of course, was already envisioning an extended future together, with presents and mortgages, comfort and routine, sex interrupted by little ones with apocalyptic nightmares, cheap child labour. He forced her to buy into the contract by purchasing a new bed, a TV ("I gave my old one away... It's a long story..."), silverware and a blender, all the indivisible accoutrements of bonded matrimony. Not because he was unsure of her feelings, but because he never thought about them, assuming incorrectly that she wanted the same things he did. He was in love, meaning all other considerations suddenly became unthinkable. He was in love, meaning everything she said came across as "I love you, too."

But Dallas wasn't ready for that again. She'd been through it already, feelings she hadn't experienced since jetting off for Sweden with the eminent physicist Dr. Ymer Framtiden. The passion. The fervour. Waiting up for him every night because she couldn't sleep without his warmth (and being *from* that northern dangler of a country, Ymer couldn't comprehend the need for more blankets), never sure if he'd even be home. For someone who dealt with time for a living, he seemed to lose track of it pretty often. In fact, she was starting to get pretty sick of all the endearing absent-mindedness, the doddering foolishness and broken dates. When he didn't return from that highly publicized voyage to the beginning of time, she... well, she...

How could she tell Marsh—was there, indeed, a delicate way to explain the actual process involved?—that she'd stopped seeing her last lover because he had burned up at temperatures the painter could not even imagine? If she interpreted Ymer's last transmission correctly, he had gone insane under the weight (no pun intended, of course; how could she joke about something so horrific? so unique and singular to her?) of too many answers. He'd discovered the first true instigation of all occurrences, and in doing so, had realized the pointlessness of his entire life's research. In the end, understanding did not provide humanity with the means for designing the future. Understanding the sequence would never provide the reasons. How could she explain that to Marsh, for whom answers were like hockey cards to be collected and traded? Exchanged?

Then Dallas started hanging out with Booting. They met at a party and quickly struck up a whispered conversation in the corner. Soon there was a project they were working on. And Marsh was fine about it while his confidence still outweighed his jealousy. But once he realized he was losing her, he found it impossible to be inoffensive, calling her at all hours of the night ("Is *he* there?"), accusing her of being a slut, waving the television remote at Booting like it was his own invention, announcing: "Hey, Booting! Look what I invented. It's a dork detector... Whoa! Stand back, big fella!" Not that it bothered Booting much. With the amputation of his leg and his loss of Judith, there was very little that could still faze him. He was so involved with destruction again, and he thought he had finally come up with a way to wipe out all art in one fell swoop. Plus, his memory was failing so rapidly he forgot about each occasion before the next was upon him; sometimes, he could barely remember Marsh. But it was the slippery slope on which Marsh's relationship with Dallas lost all traction, went horribly off course. He had no faith in her. Her employment, to him, was an exercise in frivolity and repetition, an excuse to spend time with other guys. As she spent more time at "the lab" ("You expect me to believe he's got a lab in his apartment?"), he became distrustful of her comings and goings, confronting her one night in the rain outside Booting's place, where the running water hid his tears, her coat dusty and dirty, and smeared with green down the sleeves, her hair disordered, graying, his nose sucking and blowering. She fed him some story about dining on prehistoric fish ("It was just luck, really... We had no idea what the time net might bring back..."), but he thought the tale a gaudy lie.

"A woman couldn't cover herself with that smell by rolling around with a paradox, could she?"

It was the last time they spoke. No note, no nothing. After two days, Marsh convinced the detectives to open up an investigation, but no one could figure out what might have happened after she re-entered Booting's apartment that night. No one had seen them leave. The only thing that seemed out of the ordinary when they broke down the front door was the burn marks on the kitchen floor. And the pantry tins that had been crammed with illegal, contraband radioactive materials. No one had seen hide nor hair of Booting either. Everything seemed so clear, summed up perfectly by the Chief Inspector:

"Your girlfriend... she is not your girlfriend no more..."

Dallas had somehow made him feel more realized, complete. She was what held him together. When he woke up in the middle of the night with his myriad anxieties—about accomplishment, desire, perception, rent, perpetually ignited stove burners, overfrosting refrigerators, toothy creatures gnawing at the walls, nuclear disaster, fame, success—he'd watched her sleeping (a puddle of drool collecting beneath her slackened mandible), and discovered that love was not among his fears of the future, marvelling at this wondrous beast that was woman. It was the single instance within reach of his vision of anything that had ever been alive, a body worth saving, and he wondered if he had ever been worth saving for someone else.

"There was something different about her, Burke: a drive, a spark. She was like some kind of supreme being." She was singular, his catalyst, and his base. Without her, he was doomed to hover like a lost soul, only barely touching real life before returning to Earth.

"One cannot choose but wonder," he mused. "Will she ever return?"

And Burke understood. He'd been there himself.

XXVI. Some questions, but no answers

MARSH WENT BACK home, to the coast, where he could breathe the ocean and not have to worry about making his own meals. None of his friends lived there any more. But that made things easier. There was no one to ask questions. No one to look quietly away. No one to make his story more than something he'd just imagined in his head.

Because it was the retelling that made things true.

It was the kind of Town where nothing happened. Traditional; romantic. *Ordinary*. With red-and-white paper signs pasted on the windows of the supermarket: advertising Niblets, round steak at ninety-six cents a pound (everyone knew they had sold out of *that* in the first ten minutes, but the sign remained), bananas, laundry soap, Mason jars, Jell-O, canned tuna, the most wonderful ginger cookies, cigarettes. They had no use for crime because there was no use for cash. Everyone was "good for tomorrow." The single set of traffic lights was universally considered more of an inconvenience than a safety feature. (Outside Town limits, however, it was the key bragging point.) And the churches—so many, with their stained glass homage and their beautiful, dumb ministers—stood as stationary points in time. Marsh once summed it all up: "There's a real fascination here with monotony in motion." And it was true. The only thing people ever talked about was the upcoming Bauer trial. All they ever did was fall in love. And at the end of the day, there was nothing left to do except maybe retire to your own "recovery room," take a medicinal rummy, go to the washroom, mix another drink.

A small Town like any other, shut off from the world on all sides by farmland, the ocean, a highway, and universal indifference.

And hanging over everything: a paranoia that he just couldn't shake. A deep depression that could only be held off temporarily by bags of Smarties and bottles of port. Dallas had dropped Marsh like first-period calculus, which only seemed to debilitate him further, like he was no longer even a human being, as if his position in life had been completely usurped by someone he considered less than his equal. Helpless, he retired to his old bedroom, and it was like he was lying in a wheat field, completely covered in fear and grain, just waiting for the feelings to pass or darkness to settle. He was afraid to move, because then there might be pain, or there might not be, and then he might realize that he had ceased to exist entirely.

...that he was simply playing a bit part in someone else's story.

When he returned to the City, there was a message from the Chief Inspector. The search of Booting's apartment had turned up a few things. He should probably take a look. Not only had the glazier been dealing in illegal scientific materials, but a more extensive search had revealed a mysterious stash of old stained glass windows he'd stolen from the church tower's construction site. No one could really explain the strange metallic beast in the background. They had decided it must be an angel, perhaps, a by-product of the Industrial Revolution in which the artist must have been raised, envisioning God's divine messengers as steam-powered locomotives, bearing down and chewing the earth. But more crucial to the investigation were the figures of Mary, Ruth, the angels, and the other Mary, whose resemblance to Dallas was more than a little uncanny. To the Chief Inspector, this opened the case up to a possible abduction. Booting had become obsessed with the characters in the windows, and when he'd finally come across someone who even remotely resembled them, he stalked her and took her away. They were opening the case internationally, and hoped to have some more findings soon.

"But these things often end badly, I'm afraid. This isn't television."

And Marsh nodded.

Not long after that, Burke would try to convince Marsh that the figure in the old church windows actually was Dallas. Not just someone with a passing likeness. It was her. And Marsh would have to agree there was a striking resemblance. But Burke was known for telling stories. He was looking for drama, and lately he'd begun to make less and less sense. He kept talking about evidence, and revenge, and how Truth would only be revealed once Tragedy took the stand. Poetic crap. Besides, Marsh could barely trust himself in this case. He was an artist, prone to displaying women as metaphorical ideals rather than a set of physical attributes. So he was apt to ignore the hair, the face, the figure ("Marsh, look at the size of those hands!"), and concentrate instead on the emotions, the passion of inspired creation. It was so obvious that the man who had created these windows had truly loved this woman. And Marsh didn't want to confuse those emotions with his own. He wanted to believe it might be her; because he never asked her to pose for him, he had nothing else to remember her by. But it was too much to hope for.

Dallas and Booting

XXVII. Wonmug remembers Framtiden

"THERE IS NO beginning or end. Start or finish. Just a timed loop in which everything is endlessly repeated. Riveted. Re-literated. The reiterate litany of each life's life story. A chorus too catchy to perform but once..."

Dr. Albert "Doc" Wonmug. Recently appointed Head of the Department of Speculative Quantum Mechanics (SQM) at the Universitet of Umeå. He was squarely built, balding, dressed unalteringly in his white lab coat and Coke-bottle specs, content to remain in Ymer Framtiden's eclipsing shadow forever. But when Ymer's closed timelike coaster went up in smoke (actually just the showy residual exhaust from several smoke machines; you had to do something to make people interested in science these days), Wonmug became a celebrity overnight. Suddenly, every university lecture series (at least those with SQM faculties), watch manufacturer and SciFi-Con was clambering to have him speak. And he put all his experiments on hold ("Oskar and Eva can handle everything until my return...") until his tour was through.

There were so many questions, addressing everything from the specific repercussions of this new discovery to the ultimate generalities of humanity. People wanted to know what had happened to the young physicist, wanted to make sense of a future world gone horribly wrong. How far were they from manning another test? Would Wonmug himself be volunteering? How would a time slip affect this new *FLEXtime* communication technology from Timex? What might happen, as Brian Aldiss had once prophesied, if space/time were to rupture?

Or was it possible, as some were claiming, that Framtiden hadn't gone anywhere, had simply been destroyed by a spontaneously generated black hole? Was this space anomaly a manifestation of the black hole in our hearts? Were people unsatisfied with the present? With themselves? Is that what this desire to travel in time represented?

Of course, there was very little to go on. Framtiden had left them without a guide to interpret their growing pile of civilization. After extensive searches by the university's cleaning staff, they discovered a secret cache containing several notebooks. But Ymer must have gone mad before mounting his chronic argosy, because the books harboured nothing more than a series of more or less poetic musings, mostly in the form of Minkowski diagrams and coded quantum equations, about time as an enclosed bubble chamber. In the end, he appeared to be claiming that travel in time was impossible because the same events were being constantly recycled anyway. The quickest way to reach the past was to just keep living.

This led to the popular belief that time was no longer a dimension of space, but a dimension of consciousness, a concept already made trendy by the widespread proliferation of *The Tower*. Neil Bauer was claiming to have located and proven the Origin of Thought. It said so right on the dust-jacket! Imagination was what made things real, and he could conduct the transaction on a whim. It was a concept too attractive for the public not to embrace. It returned the power of creation to the individual. Science—which everyone was afraid of anyway—became no more necessary than the ham radio, just a nostalgic reminder of another Age, those backward periods of the industrial and the technological.

It was ludicrous, of course. But Bauer had them in the palm of his hand. He could say whatever he wanted and *everyone* would listen. And so, at each presentation, Wonmug publicly mourned the passing of science and moralized on the futility of all ambition:

"I, for my own part, cannot think that these latter days of weak experiment, fragmentary theory, and lexical construction are indeed man's culminating time!"

He paused for water and dramatic effect.

"And one cannot choose but wonder... Will he ever return?"

XXVIII. A brief reflection on something even further in the past

WHEN SHE WAS growing up, nobody had ever heard of Ymer Framtiden. And then—suddenly—it seemed as though everyone was talking about him, how he came from beyond the oceans of Time and the Atlantic. What with the popularity of new scientific discoveries like anti-gravity spindizzies, the use of ribonucleic acid to increase learning efficiency, and shrink rays (often combined with robotics to perform nano-exploratory surgery, the minia-turized removal of blood clots and cancers), science con-ferences had become as sensational as movie trailers. Hugely complex computer simulations, laser light shows, gigantic inflatable puppets... All these things had become the norm rather than the exception. The annual Texas A&M Theoretical Physics Summit (in nearby College Station) was certainly no exception. And still, it was quite a surprise when the door behind the podium opened slowly, almost soundlessly, and the lights from the green room beyond were so bright they momentarily circum-scribed Ymer Framtiden in silhouette.

On first sight, Dallas imagined him as some sort of anorexic genius, so thin and pale he appeared to her. He had a queer, broad head, with a white, sincere, Scandinavian-pale face. And when he pointed his lean forefinger in her general direction (he swept the entire audience with his probing digit), she was helplessly taken by him.

She also got the eerie feeling that she'd seen him somewhere before. Which made sense, seeing as it had only been two years earlier that he'd been invited to speak at *TExtraCon*, the fan-like gathering of Texan extras in the classic film *Logan's Run*. The movie's popularity had paled in comparison to *Star Wars*, but for the inhabitants of the Lone Star city, there was nothing greater than spotting their local landmarks amid the dome city's blatant hedonism: the Burton Park Building, the big Zale HQ, even the Apparel Mart. Dallas, born only two weeks before the shooting of the film, had the role of Logan 6, son (if they could see her now!) of Michael York's title character, Logan 5. When she wouldn't look at York during the shooting of the first scene, the director decided to rewrite the script to incorporate it. It was merely the first time she would change history.

What had begun as a reunion of extras (an annual kegger at the Oz—in the film, it passed as the *Love Shop*—to relive old times) had progressed into a full-blown convention, complete with visits from all the cast excepting Logan himself. The other stars, Jenny Agutter and Richard Jordan, surely. But also the attractive young wife of Lee Majors (she kept telling everyone about her new television pilot, a show about three sexy, female cops, but no one figured it would fly), and an old guy named Peter Ustinov (who went on to host *Omni*, which was fairly cool, as well as starring as detective Hercule Poirot in several films). By the time it suited York's own interests, when he couldn't seem to land anything in the early '80s except bad TV movies, they had lost interest in him. In fact, they'd lost interest in each other. Once they had all run out of personal stories about the cast and film ("So, York turns to me and says, 'For the last time, I was not the bloody Manimal...'"), the conventioneers discovered most of them had very little in common. The unit had officially disbanded by the time Dallas reached legal drinking age, and only a small group continued to meet under the pretense of a genuine interest in science.

The only time anyone ever referred to the movie again was after the release of the 1996 television film *September*. It was the third time Agutter starred opposite York, so they decided to invite her back for old time's sake. Unfortunately, she didn't have the same effect on them as she once had. After appearing in another cult hit about werewolves, she became typecast in horrible B-flicks. The woman who had made so many adolescent boys fall in love as Jessica 6 was now the mother in *Child's Play 2*.

There was no going back.

But the eminent, young physicist Ymer Framtiden changed everything for Dallas Bright. *TExtraCon* had gone from a get-together to a fan tribute to a think tank, and eventually to a point where they were inviting actual scientists they felt had a unique vision of the future. They had invited wingnuts before: the gorilla-like Professor Challenger, Dr. Emmett Brown. But Ymer's ideas were closing in on madness. He suggested that weight displacement was crucial to gravity, even posited that the overpopulation in East-Asian countries was what kept the world on its current orbit around the sun, and that a continued emigration to North America would result in certain disaster. In fact, by the time of the Texas A&M Theoretical Physics Summit, he had rewritten relativity almost entirely, incorporating time-space as an internally fractal plane ("Not a line or a coil, but an infinite series of equally sized Russian dolls..."). He had created a tool ("...which, unfortunately, due to its nature, you can't see...") that could measure the fourth dimension with an accuracy and appropriateness beyond that of a simple clock.

He was claiming, in short, that time travel was possible. No (whispers, grunts...!), he was claiming to have done it.

Of course, after that kind of introduction, no one at the Physics Summit even felt the need to listen. They had all read Wells, Heinlein, Asimov, Niven. They knew the draw of the past rewritten. But they were equally aware of the problems time travel presented, not least of which was the potential for universal destruction. His explanation—"When the salt/alcohol compound is induced to activity through the bombardment of rays from the cosmic generator, its emanations form the basis of the complex reactions of pure and corpuscular energy by which I am able to eliminate the x, y, and z axes of space-time and hurl a material object *backward* through the layered coordinates of Time..."—was laughable. And his only proof, aside from his word, appeared to be a note he claimed to have received from the future. Through one of his un-manned time-tests. He'd sent one of his smaller prototypes ahead fifty years into the future to snap some pictures. But when it came back, someone had stuck a Post-it Note just below the lens, on which the inhabitants of that morrowing aspect of time-space had written: *We know from old records and museum models that this is the Ymer Framtiden experimental machine. Fifty years looks down on you and says, 'Good work.'*

Was this a joke?

Before he could even enter into a discussion on the physics of it all, the collected A&M scientists had already dismissed his findings as "soft science," echoing almost precisely the comments of the *TExtraCon* fanatics two years prior:

"Are you saying that we should think of time travel as being as real as ghosts?"

"Maybe time travellers *are* ghosts, wha?!"

"Don't you know that changing the past would prevent the creation of the time machine itself!"

"I guess somebody's never heard of the grandfather paradox, nyuk, nyuk, nyuk..."

Framtiden merely sighed, like the air being slowly let out of an Aharonovian balloon. After all, paradoxes could be used to argue against movement through space, insect flight, mathematics itself. Pushing through the billions upon billions of atoms in the air around us should be impossible. If they weren't willing to open their minds a little, to see past the apparent chronoclasms, there was no room for advance. Impossible?! Was the universe impossible without its cause-and-effect beginning? Was the dramatic genius of Strindberg impossible? And what about fucking Aristotle? Did he not say some four thousand fucking years ago that "Plausible impossibilities should be preferred to unconvincing possibilities?" Framtiden's findings clearly revealed a myriad of other dimensions once the others were nullified. Was the only way to convince them to go back and kill Einstein himself before he affected such a travesty of physics on mankind?

They rejected him.

And he gave them the finger from the podium and walked back to the green room, tripping over the mic cord and dumping his notes all over the stage, mumbling to himself the words that few except Dallas even heard:

"Then, feel free to believe none of it. I'm sure it makes no difference to me."

It was not the Science that attracted her to these conferences so much as the scientists themselves. Her first memories involved special effects, rocked to sleep by actors with flashing diamonds imprinted in their palms, soothed by the destructive hum of *Logan*'s killer carousel. Because of her special proximity to these films, Dallas never once considered the technicians behind the movie magic, only witnessed the pyrotechnic wonder of the film's beautiful creations. By the time she hit puberty, she was inexorably drawn to anyone in a white lab coat. So, where everyone else saw insanity in Framtiden, she saw passion. Where they witnessed him down on his hands and knees trying to re-collect his fallen notes, she imagined a close encounter of the sixty-ninth kind. By the time she'd negotiated her way back to the dressing room (the security guard was big and beefy, but she managed to keep her virtue untarnished for the real brainiac), he'd trashed the joint, set fire to the couch, put his fist through the mirror. At the last moment, she nearly turned around, but he glanced up as the door slid open, and beckoned her to come inside.

"It's all right," he chuckled, gesturing to the mess of wanton destruction around him. "I'll just go back and make sure it never happened."

Of course, he never did. Why should they benefit from the discovery they mocked like an improperly washed telescope? Idiots! Disbelievers! So many tales of the future took place in the early 21st century. It was their culture! With their cataclysmic wars. Their robotic laws,

Martian inhabitations, and utopian inadequacies! Here they were, the millennium behind them. Why was it so tough to believe, nearly a hundred years after the idea first entered human consciousness, that miracles could and did happen? And all without destroying their precarious hold on Free Will. "Temporal paradoxes are the stuff of fiction. This is real life. Sure, returning to the Past is bound to change a few things, but Time has a way of working things out. Are we so vain as to believe that we could do anything to destroy it? It's like dropping a stone into a river. The initial impact is going to cause a splash, but eventually the normal flow takes over again. Consider gravity. Or elastic tension. Soon enough, everything gets pulled tight again."

That night, back at his hotel room, they both got "pulled tight" on Absolut and OJ, popping a few Malthusian lozenges he'd picked up from another fan. But he never touched her, at least not in the way she wanted. He recognized the fact that she was a beautiful young woman, certainly, but he'd been existing so long in experimental seclusion, unable to trust anyone, that the mere proximity of any human being became purely social. He was possessed by the inexplicable need to explain everything to her. And, strangely, she wanted to accept everything at face value. Such was their immediate trust and faith in each other, over God or any theory. He was so self-assured. He spun off countless statements, unbelievable things. Everything. And although she didn't believe a word of it, she kept nodding her head anyway ("Really?"), sitting as close to him as she could ("No shit?"), their thighs in a direct contact of at least the first kind ("Is it getting warm in here?"), trying to entice him into something a bit less theoretical.

But he needed to tell someone. He'd written that whole speech and all. "We exist in a four-dimensional block universe, using time as an equal to any measurement of length, width, and breadth. Time, as just another axis of this 4-d object, projects forward and backward in both directions, not moving but always existing. The present *is*. The past *is*. The future *is*." The common belief was that time travel would be possible if matter could be pushed past the speed of light. But the question Framtiden raised was about the speed of light itself. If things began to turn back on their own time-lines as they surpassed the speed of light, what of light itself? If indeed, light's exact cruising speed was the reversal point, then light must not move through time at all. It just sat there, clinging to each and every particle of air for dear life. And even that was no good to describe it because the air was no more motion-less than a Nordic skier.

Of course, this appeared to create a paradox in and of itself. How could light be motionless, and still be moving at Einstein's speed of light, unless the speed of light was, in fact, zero?

...which meant the secret of time travel...

"Lies in not moving at all?"

Yes! That was it! He could see she understood! It was, as she could imagine, considerably more difficult than it sounded, but with a little machine he called a *kinetinull*, he found he could generate opposing compulsions to just about every acting force within a specific radius. Then, through the addition of density straps and vertigo spin pendulums, he had managed to create a perfect stasis field in which the three most common dimensions were perfectly cancelled out. Once they were removed, well, the rest was pretty simple.

Of course, all this time travel business was a bit much. Even to Dallas (she'd wait until she saw it with her own eyes). But he wasn't half-bad looking, and he made her laugh ("What did the electron say to the chemist? Quit giving out my number, you bastard!"). They had sex on the bus to the next conference (about time!), and in the morning he asked her to return to Sweden with him.

"And if you say no, I'll keep going back to ask you until you change your mind."

XXIX. A broken date

A SOUTHERN COWGIRL. A northern snowman. With the light from the meteorites entering the Earth's atmosphere bathing both their faces in an eerie glow ("Um... they're saying that asteroids are going to slam into the moon on New Year's Eve, 2023, and it could be the last night for it... Wanna go?"), he told her of his plans, and she cried into his shoulder, thinking she was losing him. "What about our date to see the *Ace in the Hole Band* at Houston's Beer Barn in 1976?" She tried to warn him: the problem with positing theories about the beginning of the universe, particularly when considering the first three minutes, was that there were so many unknowns. Time zones. The gravitational pressure of so much volatile density. The pressures of such a long-distance relationship ("Not distance, Dallas, but distemporance!"). Heaven forbid the chance that God might play a part. What if, as was quite possible, the gradual expansion of the universe did not indicate a period when the universe was also infinitely small, but that its expansion and declension were the result of a steady fluctuation like that of a sine wave? "And when, in fact, does it become technologically possible to even observe a 3°K isotropic radiation background?"

Framtiden ignored her. "Just think, Dallas," he said. "To hold infinity in the palm of your hand, and eternity in an hour. This is *my* door into summer!"

But it was so dangerous...

"Risk is a four-letter word."

There was so much they didn't know...

"Can't I have your support in this?"

What if he never came back?

"Perhaps we should fool around now then, hmmm?"

Only Dallas knew what had really happened to the Scandinavian physicist. She never released the information that she had, hidden on her body at all times, a tiny, tiny radio transmitter manufactured for her by the crafty Ymer so that they might communicate across Time like eternal Love. She was desperate for a message, a cough, anything, but she also kept it as a keepsake ("He's not coming back," Wonmug kept telling her. "Once you accept that, maybe then you can continue where he left off..."), a memory of the day her lover Ymer made his mark on history. *New Scientist*'s cover story was entitled "The Biggest Discovery: Of All Time!" *The American Physical Society*, ever cynical of the "neutral" Swedes, decried the supposed time machine's disappearance as either a trick of light akin to invisibility (the technology had been made possible years ago although never released to the general public) or a burst of energy so intense that it incinerated the entire ship in milliseconds. But the truth of the matter was that he burned up somewhere around the first minute of the universe, the temperature reaching one hundred thousand million °C, much hotter than even *Audhumla*'s specially treated hull could withstand.

Or, at the very least, he'd pulled off the biggest scientific scam in history. Dallas was never quite sure. The one time she asked him to take her with him, so she could see for herself, he stormed off into the arctic winter without looking at her:

"What does it matter now if people believe me or no? What is to come will come. And soon you too will stand aside, to murmur in pity that my words were true."

XXX. Dallas returns – mixed messages

IT WAS GIESLER who brought Dallas back from Europe to North America, on a winged bird made of dreams and hospitality, with a meal, alcohol and the occasional screened vision. And all she had to do was look nice and agree that she was sleeping with him, at an event celebrating his most successful writer to date: Neil Bauer. They had met while the overweight agent was pushing Neil's book on some Stockholm publishers, and he couldn't even explain where she'd come from. One moment he was sitting alone at the bar, and the next she had slipped through a crack in the air, sipping her vodka and orange juice. He talked her up a bit ("So a bear and a rabbit were taking a crap in the woods..."), and probably thought he was the one playing her.

"I don't have to tell you she was a hot one. Ouch!"

It was Ymer himself who eventually proposed she see other people. As the day of his departure crept closer ("Or, as the day of my arrival grows more distant..."), he began to doubt the relationship, could no longer see them together forever. He'd never been in love before ("I never had room..."), so he was never sure if the feelings he felt were the ultimate sacrifice or just some sex-induced tinglies. That was not to say he was insecure about his calculations, no, no. He was sure it would work. He'd performed too many tests to be unsure of the exact point in time at which his body would arrive. It was more a question of mental transference, awareness, memory. What if this next life he was going to proved infinitely more pleasant? Would he remember her ("Us, Ymer...!") when he was sipping his liquid mercury ("Surely we will continue to greater lengths to achieve a high as our bodies become more and more accustomed to the vices we abuse now..."), ordering his robotic poolboy to stay away from the daughter he'd generated—an experiment in genetics involving skin grafts without semen or an egg—with some diminutive woman named Weena dancing at his side. A life made perfect by the adoption of meritocracy as a governing principle. Tax breaks for the knowledgeable. Assigned occupations based on standardized IQ tests. Was it not likely that he would find the Age that was perfectly suited to him, and then decide further travel was pointless?

"It would explain the lack of time travellers in our own age."

And when he was irreversibly content, with the riddles of their own time answered, its worrisome problems solved, would he still think of her sometimes?

He shrugged. "It is by no means an irrational fancy

that, in a future existence, I shall look upon what I think of as my present existence as a dream."

But what a dream! Romantic dinners by the light of the Bunsen burners. Drinks neither shaken nor stirred, but mixed by centrifuge. Sex on a cushion of magnetic fields. How could he even risk the chance of giving that up? She was sad to see him go, but packed him a lunch of his favourites: prawns and Nutella. And when *Audhumla* blipped out of existence, the smoke from the machines hiding her tears, she tried to convince herself that he wasn't coming back. It was just easier that way. Easier than hope.

Still, the transmitter spoke to her like her innermost dreams, both reassuring and accented (just like Michael York). He was the first voice she heard when she went to bed at night; and in the morning ("Please, let me sleep just ten more minutes..."), he just wouldn't shut up. The trip, he claimed, was going slower than he thought it would. Something to do with the alcohol-based fuel un-fermenting as he travelled due to a slight tear in the tank. And yet he was still travelling backward at an alarming rate, stopping only periodically to step out and take a few snapshots. She would not have believed the crowds at the crucifixion, would have had such a great time at the invention of fire. He even promised to bring back one of the first amniotes to pull itself from the receding ocean, its stumpy paws testing the clay bank, its new lungs fit to burst with this strange thing called oxygen. Then: "Off tomorrow to the Big Bang, hugs and kisses, wish you were here, true love always..."

That fateful night, her head on the bar and her mind on other things, she ordered another Absolut ("To us, Ymer..."), scratched out a few calculations on her cocktail napkin, and heard his voice for the last time:

"...the past and future rings true..."

And then nothing. She yanked the transmitter from her cleavage, startling the fat book agent as he moved in to pounce.

The past and future rings true....!?

What could it possibly mean?

XXXI. Booting finds a new right hand

"DO YOU THINK it's true?" Booting asked them at the Grad Lounge over a game of bridge, referring to the recent rumoured breakthroughs in time travel (and remarkably not by either of the major players, Thorne and Novikov, or Sherman and Peabody, but by some relative unknown from Iceland). How else could they explain the sudden appearance of a man calling himself Enoch Soames in the Reading Room of the British Museum? Certainly there was no record of the man's existence prior to the security cameras tracking his entry into the building. He took one look at the computers, sniffed audibly, and shambled over to the least imposing librarian for assistance. Five minutes later, security was wrestling him to the ground while he tried to set fire to the card catalogue. He insisted he had come from the past. But the judge at his public mischief trial wasn't buying it. It would have been a relatively minor offense. But because he insisted on sticking with his ridiculous story, he was serving out a much longer term in a secure mental hospital. The Icelandic scientist they'd been reading about in the papers had also gone mad; at least everyone supposed so. He was never heard from again. "Can someone actually travel through time?"

"For the last time, Booting, you cannot replay the last hand."

"What if someone could surpass the speed of light?"

Dispelled once again by Marsh: "Bullshit! One of the two cosmic strings needed to generate the geometries for time travel would only trap the time machine in a shell of negative energy, a net of singularities of the same sort you'd find at the centre of a black hole, shutting off access to the time machine, and destroying the laboratory in the process. End of story."

Seemingly.

"But what if the time machine were built from the inside?"

Hmmm...

He couldn't get the idea out of his head. After his operation, Booting rarely left the house. And he'd been flirting so much with destruction again that time travel seemed the next logical step. It drove him crazy, the way they were wasting their lives. The way they made irrational decisions and actions. They were all looking toward the future with sick anticipation, so completely engrossed with the fluid succession of presents that they couldn't see the spawning creep of yesterday, how it grew with possibility every passing second while the future became shorter and bent. The future? The past *was* the future. It was the only place you could go to escape the creative drain they were currently headed down.

So, he set to work, reading everything he could get his hands on, developing sophisticated arguments ("Would any God construct a game that grew so boring so quickly?") to convince himself of the non-existence of a First Cause. Screw ontological reasoning. Existence was like a giant computer, slowly assessing every possible permutation of life until they were all exhausted: "A catalogue of all the thoughts of the mind and of all their possible combinations and divisions should represent a random encyclopaedic premonition of the Universe." There was a single point *to which* they were moving, a hopelessly boring homogeny of people and art and everything else under the sun. And this Last Effect, when the last two remaining actions collided like cosmic strings, it would repeat itself into infinity, with the slim chance—only if they were lucky—of caustic inbreeding, distorted visions like a rusting plesiosaur thrusting itself from the tar pits to replace the boring repetition they'd been stuck with.

Basically, progress had become their enemy. Imagination was like a nuclear bomb they had already dropped and they were living through the fallout. Especially where Neil was concerned. Or Burke. The poet was running around spouting such outlandish stories, about love affairs and models; success; tiny molemen and giant Greek creatures of the night. And as far as Booting was concerned, it was only a matter of time before it became the truth. Common thought stated that we couldn't imagine anything that we hadn't already experienced. Yet, if perception endured imagination, abetted it, then shouldn't the reverse also hold true? That an action or event could not occur until we had already imagined it? Essentially: "There is nothing that human imagination can figure that human genius and skill cannot aspire to realize." Or rather: "Whatever is imaginable is possible." In fact, it was probable. Burke's kind of overactive imagination was leading to chaos, a breakdown of the temporal and its fabrics, the boundaries of the imaginable demolishing the walls of the desirable. And the only way to save themselves? The path *never* travelled. Through time.

It was in the past, if only they could reach it, that they would uncover more and more causes, an infinite number of original ideas as they dribbled from the giant crack of Time. It was the path to eternal life, to new life every day, and not a story that ended among dead bodies in the vaults of a castle, like Neil's.

Even Neil recognized it. "We must emerge from the recesses of futurity," Booting paraphrased what he thought the writer had said the night he gave him the manuscript for safe keeping. "Moving backward we cannot die."

And Booting wasn't speaking figuratively any more. He'd adopted the life of the Philosopher, the Inventor, and the Philosophical Investigator, which led him to frequent rants on subjects like temporal transience. Or infinite levels of dimensionality. Not that the rest of them understood what he was getting at. They never had. Never would. Instead, they chose to listen to Neil, The King of the Fictionary, The Lord of List-erature, who took the microphone at his own book launch and said, "I project a new canon. I will reject the laurels of my nation. And I expect to walk down the street and spit on people without recourse." Or they let their lives be shaped by Marsh, who had volunteered to work the door at the same launch and handed out name tags with punchlines from his repressed childhood (Alfred Hitchcock, Englebert Humperdink, I. P. Overbridge, Inspector Boobies), and had already scratched out Hugh Jazz for Booting, but the glazier waved him off and hobbled straight by:

"So many people make a name nowadays that it's more distinguished to remain in obscurity..."

The only person who seemed to listen to him at that party was Dallas. And when he saw her across the room, he could barely control himself. He felt himself growing pale, and a curious sensation of terror came over him. What a laugh she had! Just like a thrush singing. And how pretty she was in her cotton dress and large hat! It was all he could do to say the first things that came into his head ("Sometimes I think I can even feel something, but I'm never sure, when I do it myself, if it's in my leg or my hand..."), but she made him feel so comfortable, and before he knew it, he was rambling on about chronic argonauts, and Nebogipfel's Theorem, and the stories he'd heard about the Way-Bac Machine, supposedly invented in the '60s, which he couldn't quite believe because they were filled with such inconsistency. Most of the calculations seemed plausible, he told her, but so much of it was immature and fantastic, equal space devoted to talking dogs, experiments with young children, punnish allusions to fairy tale and history. There were times, he almost cried, when this sort of thing made him doubt what he was doing.

"And still," he continued, "how can you not believe in it? In 1949, Kurt Gödel published solutions to Einstein's general relativity gravitational field equations that suggested the possibility of time travel, even to the past! It's like inventing the steam engine. Surely someone would create a car by now."

And, good Lord, he could see she understood.

XXXII. The time machine

WHAT COULD SHE do? Although Dallas began to care deeply for him, she and Marsh were from such different worlds. He approached her interests as metaphors for his own art (humanity's dance with science, or the poetic curse of nostalgia), but rarely made the effort to genuinely understand what she was telling him. When she tried to talk about Framtiden's work, he tried to deflate it with his easy self-assuredness: "There are no paradoxes in physics. Only in our attempts to understand physical ideas by using inadequate reasoning or false intuition." And then he would just start with the airbrushing, constructing futuristic utopias under glass, or dead planets of barren rock hiding fantastic underground societies, and always with an improperly restrained, impossibly busty heroine. The futuristic machines he designed for her were things of imagination and innovation: sleek rockets with gracefully sloped wings and fins, rockets blazing, able to surpass the speed of light through advanced meta-aerodynamics; huge, spinning wheels, with blades that sworped and clathered through time's barriers; or, most improbable, an upright Escherian box, with only one carefully moulded side (neither an inside nor an outside), able to slip easily into other dimensions because of its Möbial relation to space; but Marsh's fantastic designs were hardly prepared for the harsh realities she was proposing, where what was truly needed was a contraption like a sterile needle, able to pass through things without lesion, with an elastic rigidity, a weightless mass, not to mention substances able to withstand incredible heat. Not that she wanted to talk about work when she got home, anyway. They only ended up fighting.

M: "You know, the only time I ever get mad at *you* is when *you* get mad at *me*. What's *your* fucking excuse?"

D: "I really don't want to talk about this now..."

M: "Excuse me for being interested in your job."

D: "Puzzles, you mean. You don't give a shit about my job."

M: "Whatever..."

D: "And it's not like you ever listen to my answers, anyway."

M: "Blah, blah, blah..."

Not that she trusted Booting immediately. No, there was definitely something unstable about him. But there were a few things that he said that first night that made her trust him enough to visit his apartment a few days later. He seemed embarrassed when he greeted her at the door, like she was his first crush and he was finally getting up the nerve to ask her out. But he still managed to get a few words out through his distraction. He offered her tea.

"Where is it?" she said.

The proof he claimed he had.

And he showed her the windows.

It was true. In the features of the holy matriarchs, she saw nothing but her own reflection, hands you could hide a horse behind, the same flaming Texan sunset hair. Booting had done some research into the artist, but aside from designing these particular windows, he was perhaps most known for being one of the sole survivors in the diphtheria epidemic of 1853. And little was mentioned about his source of inspiration. Even less was made of the abrupt change in style he adopted for the church, or of his decision to retire from glazing after he awoke from the diphtheria fever, still coughing up blood, and found he was still alive. All Booting knew was this was a sign. She was the key.

And she agreed.

It was as though they were meant for each other, two people who believed in physics and knew that the distinction between past, present, and future was only a stubbornly persistent illusion. She seemed to understand so much, to grasp the concepts so readily: time not as a tightly coiled spring, but as a succession of equal dimensions. She even accepted temporality as a kind of spirit world all around them, in this dimension, an angle they had never been trained to perceive. They spent long hours together, closed up in his apartment, debating the designs of Gott, Morris, and Thorne, analyzing Hawking's apparent defection to the side of the Believers, and tracing diagrams and equations on the wall in indelible ink, with Dallas playing the role of skeptic and Booting driving her forward.

"Of course, there are no closed timelike curves if the space-times have physically accepted our global structure..."

"If there were some way to electrically suppress those quantum fluctuations..."

Most importantly, they helped each other believe by explaining away the unpleasantness of uncertainty, the apparent inconsistencies, not to mention the logical arguments of people like Bagnall and Untermeyer. If time travel were possible, how come there weren't any travellers visiting the beginning of this century? Too boring. What would happen if a painter from the past was shown his future masterpieces before their actual creation? Who cares? And what about the grandfather paradox? Just another way of looking at things. Essentially, if time travel were possible, there would be an infinite number of "possible worlds," alternate realities, each as valid as the last. Different relationships, places where gravity was not so grave, or flung you from the Earth due to the planet's spin.

They would make the machine together. Booting's original plans were not entirely dissimilar to Framtiden's, certainly more theoretical than scientific and yet still making use of the latest findings: Logan and Preston; Beckett and Calavicci. Miraculously, the actual jump theory was almost identical, based on three gyrostats, three perpendicular planes of Euclidean space, each made of ebony cased in copper, a perfect gyrostatic cube that would maintain stability in space impossible for the average human. Around that were rods of tightly rolled quartz ribbons set in quartz sockets, and semicircular suspension forks made of nickel, everything powered by a special stationary bicycle (propped up by Neil's original manuscript to keep it level, thank God it was good for something!), with a special prosthetic pedal for Booting's missing limb. If he could maintain x, y, and z as constants, only then could he begin to manipulate the delicious w, unlocking the *when* and *whip* and *wish* of time.

But it was Dallas's experience that would prove crucial to his success. Booting had constructed the outer shell from albalune mouldings (a by-product of moondust that had superceded most woodwork and ceramic tiles years ago), thinking it would be enough protection no matter what temporal weather he encountered. They'd been using it in the space program for their Venus missions, and they'd chosen it over the other materials in the Iridio-Aluminoid family. But for Dallas it was the same story, the uncertainty of the pre-universe monobloc, that first second made crazy with exploding mesons and freequarks, everything rushing by in metronomic beats. If lunarium didn't hold, could they trust anything else from that God-forsaken satellite? Especially when confronted with the temperature at the beginning of time itself?

"Who wants to see that shit anyway?"

For her, that was part of the deal.

She was going after Framtiden.

So, they went back to the drawing board, re-examining the issue of heat and integrity. Using a special computer program Dr. Wonmug had written to simulate the universe's pre-expansion temperatures, they subjected each element to hours of exposure. And the final breakthrough came when they tried Booting's earlier invention of a glass impervious to heat of any sort. It was difficult to mould properly, and so the outer shell of their machine resembled a translucent, lumpy mass (from a distance, it gave off a blue metallic sheen), but it took anything Wonmug's synthesizer could toss at it. They climbed inside. And he depressed the crystal button, both of them pedalling for all they were worth.

XXXIII. 'To that first nothing under earth.'

THE FEELING WAS one Booting would always be at a loss to describe. Not a blade, not an insect, which spoke of the present, was between him and the past. And suddenly, everything was known. The search for lost things was only hindered by Time. Not memory, which was knowledge removed from the moment of actual knowing. Nor regret: knowledge mangled by wishful thinking. Just Time.

The problem was they became caught in a loop, the same events recurring endlessly through time. They were slowing down directly before the big event (a crucial variable Framtiden neglected to include in his own equations), hoping to use the reverse gravity of the universe's epicentre to propel them back to fame and fortune. But as most simple theories are, it was also flawed. Once Dallas and Booting had witnessed that ultimate paradoxical beginning of the universe, the numbers ceased to make sense. They inverted upon themselves once they equalled zero exactly, and in the seconds directly before the Bang (an impossibly negative existence, before their ship passed through the universe's impossibly constipated rectum), the time travellers were thrust into an imaginary physics more complex than the quantum world of the late 20th century. On the return trip, they were confronted by an endless number of their immediate selves, repetitive insurgencies of awareness.

All Time was compressed into that tiny pre-explosion universe, and all possibility weighed down on them like a rolling pin.

At that moment, they were every moment, every person. Trapped, they had done everything. Had existed for all eternity. (Which also held true for Neil's manuscript, propped under the back leg of their brilliant beast.) Booting and Dallas never found any verifiable trace of Framtiden or *Audhumla*. But hovering just outside the monobloc, as Booting signed his name on the kernel of the universe, something passed them, a vehicle shaped like a cow's underbelly. Booting wondered ("Do you think...?"). Dallas sighed ("Hmmm..."). Then there was a flash from within the monobloc as everything suddenly closed in upon itself, and the cosmos rumbled with an impending sneeze.

"Let's get outta here."

"You got it."

Denouement

XXXIV. The art of absence

AFTER DALLAS, ALL the women Marsh met looked the same. Could this have been what Framtiden was getting at? Was this the way history repeats itself? Of course, he was also drinking quite heavily in those days, looking to dilute his sorrow, trying to shut out the rest of existence. Marsh was both painter and photographer, constantly aware of his own visual image, more acclimatized to tragic respect than pity. So he would stake out his own corner of the Grad Lounge, chastise the waitress when the rum did not appear on time ("Time is not a luxury, but a conceit..."), and pretend to read up on photography ("See? I'm fine!") while scoping the mags for nudes. Then—sweet, fair, rum gods—he would see her face on some rich debutante and forget about the rest of them. When they reached his loft, he didn't even detour to the stereo as he used to, just immediately started fumbling for the bra clasp. He wanted to be in love again. But only with Dallas. And undressed, the illusion was gone. It was only some small part of them that reminded Marsh of her. A grinning eye crease. A tiptoed sway. The subtle trace of white cranial fallout about the shoulders. When the panties of that rich one hit the floor, he fingered her absently, but his heart wasn't in it, and she eventually shipped off for the dorm.

Her parting words: "See you later, Spaceman! I thought your kind was, like, into Earth chicks?"

They came and they went, passing through his life like the ticking of the days, each representing some facet of what he had lost with Dallas. And because he couldn't bring himself to have sex with them, he started drawing them, a return to portraiture, where the scientific nature of his more recent experiments was replaced by the simplicity of replication. It was an artistic form of therapy for him; the grid emerged simply from frustration. In his second-floor studio, with the spotlights excessively bright, he explored every angle of the female form, subjecting his models to hours of gruelling, motionless stasis. They were asked to hold positions impossible to maintain. Or conversely, to perpetuate continuous movement (if he had spotted them dancing). And they were often so exhausted by the end of it that they remembered little of their experience. Not that this troubled him much, but the sketches suffered for it, took on a blurred effect. So he started taking photos, rushing the models back onto the street as quickly as possible so he could get back to the drawing board, mapping each image in a set of intersecting vertices. It was a means to greater levels of realism, yet also a way to break down the women he drew. Each pose became identical, so that the grids could be manipulated like huge, complex, *exquisite corpses*. One square interchangeable with the corresponding quadrant in any other. The building blocks for regained love.

And gradually, as absence began to take over as his driving force, the space between his lines began to fade. He would see the hint of something behind each irrelevant scratch and smudge, and would ponder the images trapped beneath. The absolute silence of presence. He believed it might have been Beckett who said that the best music was the music that became inaudible after a few bars (someone should have told that to Burke's ex, Anne-Sophie), and that similarly, the object that becomes invisible before your eyes is, so to speak, the brightest and best. So he used progressively harder pencils, until his ghost-like renderings were as faint as day-old odours, more like memories than depictions. He selected models that weren't nearly as stunning. Models who were less *there*. And he absently reproduced them in mass quantities without thought of the repercussions, leaving no inch unmarked, paying no attention to his own markings but what lay underneath.

Judith failed repeatedly to understand his experiments. He was achieving new levels of realism through his complex pattern of grids and photomapping, but she could never keep up her part of the bargain: keeping still. For someone who claimed to have lived surrounded by colour on a daily basis (it had taken quite a few cosmetic surgeries to remove the effects of Venn's fetish, hours and hours under electrolytic knives, bleaching douses, laser grafts), she failed daily to comprehend its basic tenets. So he kicked her out. Christ! He wasn't talking about things that just looked futuristic: metallic, shiny, blue spaceships; mercury fountains (like millions of liquid BBs in shimmering cascade); tinfoil automatons. Not any more. He was proposing an entirely new form of Art, a study of what was missing ("The spaces left behind by the bleeding souls of objects and people passing into another existence…"). If there were sounds they could not hear, what about colours that were invisible to the human eye? Chemists had already detected actinic rays, integral components of light that human beings were unable to discern. He would paint in those colours.

"The human eye is an imperfect instrument, Judith. Its range is but a few notes on the real chromatic scale."

To which she could only respond with past boyfriends, how one of her early lovers had conducted similar experiments in his off-white laboratory (a beige so faint that it was indiscernible to most eyes, maintaining the illusion of sterility, but just enough tint to subdue his albuphobia). He was always talking about new colours, my God, like how, if colour were the refraction of light rays back at the eye, couldn't those light rays be completely turned around, forced into an endless loop of chromatic paradox, in effect, invisibility…

And Marsh (who never really listened, anyway, but made a special point not to be concerned with the past, didn't even catch the bit about selling the secret to the *American Physical Society*): "I am not mad! There are colours we cannot see!"

Ironically, the answer seemed to lie with Isabella. He was completely uninterested in everything that emerged from the girl's mouth, including her lips. But whenever he tried to think of her, he could remember so little that he knew she was his new perfect model. He'd barely noticed her when they lived together, her presence was microscopic. With the proper pencils, he could have worked on her all day and still come up with nothing. So, the next night Marsh showed up at Isabella's new place over the bowling alley.

"There's this great movie on TV, and you have my set..."

Then, perhaps even more carefully, he started erasing, steadily un-creating until only the lines of the grid remained, removing any detail he felt undefining of the subject in question. Isabella accused him of no longer knowing what his subject was. And eventually, he abandoned all pretense of representation, concentrating solely on new divisions, tighter grids, splitting each square vertically and horizontally to produce four more boxes, over and over, repeatedly quadrupling the number of focus sets without increasing the surface area of the whole. His theory was that as he magnified each grid through repeated quadration, something might emerge from the absence, that the increase in volume might reach a breaking point where the vacuum turned in on itself. As each quadrate was dissected into its four counterparts, there would eventually be too many "spaces" to be seen by the naked eye. The absence would begin to disappear through sheer volume, the empty spaces overtaken by their conjoined borders, the lines. In that instant, his huge canvasses encrusted with graphite, he thought the leaving—the creation of the absence—would be reversed, and Dallas might return.

XXXV. The physical anomalist's nightmare

WHEN ANNE-SOPHIE died (the papers all mentioned a drug overdose, although the body was never found), Nästa moved from one freaky chick to another, logging hours as an itinerant boyfriend on the North American circuit. Over the red lands and the gray lands, twisting up into the mountains, crossing the Divide and down into the bright and terrible desert, and across the desert to the mountains again, and into the rich California valleys, he dragged his cello from roadhouse to roadhouse, just hoping for another meal and a place to lay his head. His show went back to his early days, inflicting various degrees of pain upon himself as he played. A fire beneath his chair. Repeatedly scratching the same patch of skin. Members of the audience were asked to hit him in the stomach as hard as they could. He dropped large, heavy objects on foot and hand. More than once he took a cannonball to the groin. Then one night, after tripping home behind a waitress with webbed fingers and toes (as per usual, she approached him after the show, swooning, "I never had thought to meet sum'n like me in

Amarillo..."), it all caught up with him, when her real boyfriend came home suddenly with a group of his drinkin' buddies, finding them poking fingers into each other's wounds in the bathtub, opting to see if the little freak could survive several boots to the head, a crack to the ribs, a knife in his side. Nästa broke someone's nose with the neck of his cello, but there were altogether too many of them. And despite the protests of his aquatic lover ("Leav'm alone! He weren't hurtin' no one!"), they would not relent. He was different ("Them goddamn freaks got no sense and no feeling. They ain't human..."), and smaller.

XXXVI. Mother and child

THEY STOPPED TO recalculate. Booting went off for help ("Wonmug, maybe?"). But the glazier mistakenly abandoned Dallas with his unborn child in a world where she could not easily fend for herself, leaving her trapped in a Newtonian universe of bruised apples and Creationists. He would never find her again. He would actually never find anything again. The owner of the nearby home, awoken by the sounds of overexcited clucking in the hen house, burst into the barn where Booting had hidden her, his musket unshucked, found her feverish in a drench of blood and amniotic fluid, his horse sniffing at the placenta.

Almost coincidentally, he was a glazier, too. He was good to her. He took her into his own home, and was so inspired by her beauty that he used her as the model for all of his work, in particular a commission to design and create the windows for the new church they were building. He even included the strange metallic machine he'd seen out on the marshes several nights prior to finding her. They were married in that same church, under the auspices of God and Dallas's own images, and later she and her son both died of simple diphtheria, mother and child, amen, which they could so easily have cured in her own age with a simple vaccination. Their bodies were buried in the catacombs beneath the church.

XXXVII. A reconsideration

"I JUST DON'T know if I can spend my life with a writer,"
Judith said, which Neil misinterpreted as a judgment on
his choice of career rather than on his entire being. He
thought it was something he might be able to change. He
didn't need to do it, he told her. He could find other ways
to express himself. He had found some small satisfaction
in teaching, perhaps he could develop that? When they'd
first met, he told her she would always play second fiddle
to his book. If it came down to a choice ("What choice?
It's not like you'd have to move somewhere to be a more
successful writer?"), he'd leave her. But that had been so
long ago, before he really knew her. He'd discovered what
was really important, which was love. And if you had love
the rest didn't matter, couldn't she see that? What was the
point of dreams and success if you had no one to share
them with? So he was willing to give it all up, to abandon
fiction, with all its insight, its ardent ways, smoke of praise,
and its whining ivory; it was for the noble, which he was
not, the intensely desirable, which he could only aspire to
be. No more dreams, no more fun, he would give up all the

heavenly frustration and neurosis, just to be with her, to be what she wanted, to be...

Judith looked away. "I wouldn't want you to do that."

So Neil said, "Nothing I say can change the way you feel, so I guess you'll have to decide that for yourself."

"I guess so."

And they spent the next week unsure. Unsure of themselves and unsure of each other. Or, rather, Neil was sure of his own feelings, but he wasn't going to divulge them without some sort of sign from her. And Judith was also fairly certain, but she didn't want to come out as the bad guy. So they continued to live as if nothing had transpired between them. They ate together, watched television together, slept in the same bed without touching. When he asked her if she wanted to go to the Grad Lounge for dinner, she agreed, and when he met her on the subway platform, she hugged him without speaking, spoke once again without looking at him:

"I want to try."

"I'm glad."

Burke and Micheline

XXXVIII. Building a tower out of words

ALL HE WANTED was to fall in love before he died. He wanted to meet someone who understood him, who wanted to be understood, and who didn't push him away in the middle of the night because the heat came over her like a sense of unknown dread. He wanted to meet someone spontaneously, and perhaps not even notice at first that he was falling in love. Just carrying on a casual conversation at the Grad Lounge, with the friend of someone Marsh was trying to sleep with, until they realized it was time to go, and that the bar staff was ushering everyone out the door, and that Marsh and this other girl were practically spread out on the pool table, and that they had suddenly started kissing.

"Maybe we should kiss, too."

And they would.

And then it would be one of those horrible, tragic deaths; like being buried alive with only a small tube to the surface for air, and the humidity attracts more and more earwigs until it's no longer possible to suck another molecule of air around them; or succumbing to a viral paralysis that leaves you alert but immobile while your starving dogs start at your legs and work slowly upwards; or as part of an unsolvable murder-suicide (two words stabbed mutually in the side by a sharpened hyphen), with both of their bodies too mutilated to be shown on television.

Not just an old man in a hospital bed, with more holes in him than when he started out in life.

Like the tube they punched in the side of his neck because his arms are all used up with other tubes, which he'd like to believe is some new kind of steroid that will cause him to instantly bulk up to enormous sizes and send him on a crime spree of unimaginable proportions, but he's been told it's actually just for hydration.

Or the spot where they'd opened him up to insert the pacemaker.

Or the ostomy bag to the right of his belly button, because prostate cancer led to colon cancer led to rectal cancer led to a bunch of student doctors peering down at his hairy butt while the lead surgeon explained the various stages of the disease's *occupation* (that's the word they use), and how they had to remove a sizeable piece of his large intestine and sew his real asshole shut.

And tear him a new one.

Micheline assured him, he wasn't dying.

"We're all dying."

Well, he certainly wasn't old. He would get over it.

"Never!"

Besides, what did she know? She had no imagination to speak of, was a model used to creating the realities that others set out for her, was able to accept whatever kind of world was placed in front of her. Meanwhile, Burke was stuck in another time, constantly travelling back to the family situation of his earlier childhood, where he imagined his parents as faultless relationship pioneers. And before Micheline, he ruined each of his relationships by trying to make them measure up. Burke was sure the girl that he met during his frosh week—a business major with nothing special about her but also nothing terribly wrong—was going to be the one, at least for the first few days when he found it almost impossible to find her again. This was Burke's nature. He made real life out of stories, living a million other lives in his head that were no more or less real than the things he saw with his eyes. He made things out of words, and it was altogether easier when she wasn't around to disturb him. For that short time, he was actually able to imagine the future, witnessing every possible happiness that could arise from their union, including the one where they took frequent trips to the country, camping on provincial lots surrounded by families of five and screwing haphazardly under the sonic cover of the motorboats on the lake. A few blocks off the main drag, in a town named after a hockey player, they would find the hospital, deserted and wheezing, with a huge For Sale sign fallen over on the front lawn. Who would buy a hospital? They would! And they'd have a hundred and fifty kids to fill every single room.

"What about us?"

Of course. One hundred and forty-nine, each with a random grouping of letters and numbers for a name, taken from the first one hundred and forty-nine licence plates to drift by once they'd signed the deed.

But then he saw her walk by when he was eating breakfast with some friends.

And he ran after her to see if she might want to go out for dinner sometime.

And his imagination was no match for when, tragically, she said yes.

XXXIX. The pungent contradiction of the general idea

THEN HE MET Micheline...

Burke liked to tell the story (different from Micheline's own, and different from some of the other stories he invented when discussing his own biography) about how he and Micheline first met. "It was an ambrosian metaphor," he said, by which he meant, he told them, expounding the story, drawing it out, only more poetically, that they met in the produce section at the supermarket, surrounded by zucchini, and bananas, and melons, and avocados, and artichoke hearts. When he saw her standing in the express lane, surrounded by the French camera crew and adoring sycophants, he nearly dropped the eight items or less that he had balanced precariously in the crook of his arm. Spotting her photo on the cover, he hastily added *Cosmo* to his pile. But the Paris crew complained that he now had too many *objets d'aliment*. And Micheline, dressed tastefully—the look of the year was casual—in jeans and a brown corduroy shirt, said she would buy one of the items for him, and reached for his boneless chicken breasts...

Flashflashflashflash... The camera crew went wild...

"And maybe she doesn't look like a model now," Burke added as a postscript, patting her hand affectionately, "but in her day, she graced the runways of Paris and Rome, was the spokesmodel for CoverGirl *and* Estée Lauder. She had the politicians holding their crotches, the priests whipping themselves into apostasy, little boys around the world hitting puberty before they hit double digits. But those were the old days..."

...which was ridiculous, because they could all see she still had it. Her teeth were still like beacons. She didn't look like she'd grown a day older. The years they'd been together had been airbrushed from her timelessness. It was just Burke. Still a poet, he lived in the past where his memories were better than the present moment out of necessity. More vivid, more crucial. They all understood, and forgave.

Besides, the story was still a romantic one, full of strange meetings and stolen photographs, and a hint of sex and nudity, even if it were coded in poultry and produce, or on the cover of a magazine. And whereas the others were constantly finding themselves in states of discordance (Marsh's girlfriend had run off with one of his best friends, and it looked as though Neil might have killed Judith after all), Burke and Micheline's world was without conflict. Instead of fighting, they looked deep into the other's eyes, found once again what they were searching for, and went quietly to bed.

They were married in the church beneath Booting's new windows: pleasant, abstract shapes that announced the Word of God. And the ceremony was simple. All-encompassing. With Burke's lofty hopes and ideals, yet practical like Micheline. Her dress had been donated by Vera Wang, a saucy but sophisticated number in duchesse satin, with a stylishly subversive inverted veil covering only her eyes, the neck low-cut for the *In Style* photographer, carrying a nosegay of black beauty and red garden roses interspersed with red pepperberries. And at the reception, they feasted on lobster and celery sticks, in honour of their respective backgrounds, while the rest was all extravaganza. Both Marsh and Burke's father claimed to be friends of the bride, and sat wedged between six-foot Amazons in swimsuits and lingerie. And they wrote their own vows.

"I promise."

A nod of agreement.

For one afternoon, Burke seemed on top form. Suddenly it seemed as though his dreams were coming true. Everyone agreed it was one of the most beautiful weddings they'd ever attended. The only time he really faltered was when Booting came running up to him at the reception and pushed his unwrapped gift at them, winking at Micheline.

"Sorry I'm late," the glazier sneered, scanning the flock of models from across the room. "Nice buffet."

"Your leg..." Burke muttered.

"Shit, did I spill something on my pants...?"

And from that point onward, it was easy to see that Burke was distracted, disconsolate, his imagination unable to keep up with so much of the mundane and predictable. He had made such a play at understanding Life, and once he felt he had gained a grasp on it, it had allowed him to complete the boring reality of their lives with whatever he saw fit. But like his own imaginary relationships, so much of it relied on absence. And suddenly, here they all were. Booting, his stomachy gut leathering out over his belt, exchanged tasteful jokes with the minister by the buffet. Marsh kept his eyes on the floor, Isabella squeezing his arm in careful reminder. And Neil and Judith received congratulations near the bar, Judith grown unstable and ugly with child. It made no sense to him. When it came time to cut the cake, Burke slipped outside for a cigarette with Marsh.

...which was when Marsh mumbled something about rising interest rates, or mortgages, and the world Burke had created around them came tumbling down. "Is this the life you wanted?" he attacked the ex-painter. "Settling into the predictability of the believable?" Where, he asked Marsh, was the unrealistic bliss of the extraordinary? Where was the beauty? Was all life really without a compelling story?

"What do you mean, anyway," Marsh asked surlily, "by prating about beauty and imagination in this miserable God-forsaken hinterland?"

"..."

"Not everybody's beautiful, Burke. Not like in your little world."

"They could be."

"They wouldn't want to be."

XL. Death of the Grammar Architect

OF COURSE, NO one—not even Micheline—realized it was just his poetic nature reaching full maturity, confusing his speech in metre and metaphor. He still understood everything they said, and their words dwelt inside his head like harboured nuts. It was just that his own words came out like beautiful, broken-necked birds, spinning futilely on gusts of symbolic twisters. Or they formed an incomprehensibly rigid universe, his words dropping one onto the next with ever-increasing speed, like the flapping of a dead wing.

"Something's missing," he muttered.

And he disappeared into the kitchen.

There was an emptiness. A void. Mostly Burke felt like he was vanishing, or that everything around him was getting less and less memorable, and Micheline became more and more important. He was alone, susceptible to chronic bouts of binge poetry; he was unheeded (even his publisher seemed to have lost interest in him), unhappy and near to the wild revenge of life; the tediums of the everyday held him like a deserted beach.

For Burke, the world had ceased to make sense. Maybe it was because he was growing older (only with age did time seem to move forward, instead of squatting idly over the squalid shitpile of history they called *the present*). Or perhaps this was what happened when one fell in love. But the world he knew was quickly being left behind. He had assimilated another life into his own (he flipped through her photos in the Sears catalogue; she was appearing in another Doritos commercial where she had one line), and in so doing (her parents were utter bores, government employees with unreasonable demands), he had been forced to accept a world bogged down by basic actions. The everyday. He had become surrounded by impossibly boring theories, a deductive reasoning dissimilar to his own speculative existence, and the stories he lived had become less centred around the fantastic, more focused on practicality.

He was living out of time, outside his normal scope of existence.

As were they all.

His imagination could no longer keep up.

And then, one day, Burke caught sight of Anne-Sophie on the street. Nästa wasn't with her. But it was so easy to see they were still together. She was so much more outgoing. Unconcerned with the impression she made on others. She apologized for not maintaining contact, said she had heard he was happy and that she was glad to see it with her own eyes, to tell him there were no hard feelings, that they could still talk and possibly hang out occasionally, especially now that they both had other people in their lives...

But wasn't it too late to come crawling back? Here in this place? She'd put on weight. Several tons, to be precise. Mostly in strange metals most people had never heard of. Not dead yet, no, but still an abomination. After she left him, Burke spent nearly a year alternating between hate and pity, and had finally settled on disassociation because it was easiest. He asked her how the freak show was going.

"Why, Burke, do you not understand? Why must you do this? These stories? I tour with an opera company now. Nästa is my manager." She looked so good. Happier. She ran a finger along her delicate throat. "Why you cannot accept the truth?"

The truth? When he asked her if she had slept with Nästa before leaving him, she refused to answer. And he knew the truth.

But if the truth was what she wanted then, well, fine. The truth. The truth was that he felt no luckier moment than when he avoided spending the rest of his life with her. The truth was that he had taken many great things from their relationship, but not one was having known her. The truth was that he had no good memories of the relationship because they were all so tainted by his current disappointment in her. The truth was that she was not the sweet innocent everyone else supposed her to be. And the truth was that he could have forgiven everything except her claim that she really did want to stay friends when she had no intention of doing so.

So...

"How've you been?"

"Fine." She asked him if he were still writing poems.

"About whom?" he shot back.

"Well, I guess it doesn't matter, really."

No, he supposed not, and felt badly for having been mean with her. What if he had judged her harshly? If her life were a simple rosary of hours, her life simple and strange as an opera singer's life, a sopranic bird, restless all day, cranky at sundown? Her heart simple and willful as a simple, cranky, sopranic, beautiful seabird's heart? And not just her, but the others as well. He'd spent so much time and energy constructing complicated motivation in their lives. These strange *other-lives*. To make sense of it. But maybe they had never had reasons for what they did. Not even an idea that things were wrong. Just an instinct that something wasn't right. And how could he fault them for that? Fault her? He was reminded of a discussion they had had about fear and logic in the motivation process of actions, how he had broken down in her arms, and how she had held him as he cried out loud against the injustices of art.

"But what frustrates me most now, Sophe, is that the thing I fear the most, and which seems to make the most sense, is the one thing I won't do..."

"Ah... here is the drama..."

There was no beginning or end. Start or finish. Just every-thing, always.

Nothing came before anything else.

They were all happening simultaneously.

And over Ymer's shoulder, a small flame, the tiniest flickering thereof. A breach in the hull to match the tear he'd made in space-time. Audhumla was still gathering speed. Ymer was still too driven. There was nothing more important than this moment. Than knowing.

But off the starboard bow, he caught a glimpse of something else. Not a star, but lit from within. And not spread over time-space like everything else, but three-dimensional like him. He pressed his hand to the glass, and breathed slowly into the radio...

The past and present rings, true love, for you and me, calling...

Chris Eaton, Toronto, 2005